# A PLACE FOR DAYDREAMS

ROSEWOOD BEACH BOOK THREE

FIONA BAKER

## JOIN MY NEWSLETTER

If you love beachy, feel-good women's fiction, sign up to receive my newsletter, where you'll get free books, exclusive bonus content, and info on my new releases and sales!

# CHAPTER ONE

Dean Owens shut the door to his office and took a deep breath. Through the window, he could see the charming Main Street of Rosewood Beach, his hometown on the shores of Connecticut. A few of the trees that bordered the sidewalk were already starting to flush with the first warm colors of autumn. He watched a dried leaf scuttle across the sidewalk in a gust of wind, and he glanced up at the cloudy sky, wondering if it might rain.

He sighed and sat down in the comfortable swivel chair behind his desk. He could hear the sound of his employees still working hard on cars out in the garage of his auto repair shop, and he winced a little, wishing he was still working with them. He always felt bad about taking breaks, especially so late in the workday like this, but his hands were throbbing and his chest felt heavy with fatigue.

He leaned his head back and closed his eyes, remembering what it had been like to work a full day of work before his diagnosis with osteoarthritis. He'd gotten tired, but not like this. There was the almost pleasant fatigue that came with long hours of physical exertion, and there was the cold, achy fatigue that he was feeling at the moment.

He smiled wryly, reminding himself that things could be a great deal worse. He had a lot to be thankful for. He owned the auto repair shop, business was booming, and he had smart, capable employees who did their jobs well. In addition to that, he had a wonderful family who made him happy every day.

Despite how busy they all were from balancing their personal lives with running the family restaurant, The Lighthouse Grill, they always found time to be with one another and offer support and encouragement. His twin sister Hazel was especially caring, and often made him and the other mechanics a batch of cookies.

He smiled, thinking about how when his sisters Alexis and Julia had come back into town for their father's funeral, he'd expected them to return to their homes in New York and Los Angeles soon afterward.

Instead, Julia had stayed to date a young single father named Cooper Harris, and Alexis had found herself wanting to stay in her hometown rather than return to an empty L.A. mansion and a distant husband. Now that Alexis's husband Grayson had moved to Rosewood Beach to show her how committed he was to revitalizing their marriage, it seemed that everyone in the Owens family was in Rosewood Beach to stay.

He felt grateful that his family had been there when he'd first learned of his condition. Although he hadn't wanted to tell them about it right away, he knew that it was their love and support that had enabled him to stay positive in spite of the new and unexpected difficulties he was experiencing.

He'd expected them to take it hard and start treating him differently, and he hadn't wanted to face that right away. However, although they'd been sad, they were also determined to keep his spirits lifted, and that helped greatly. They also encouraged him to slow down and take breaks, and although it wasn't something he wanted to do, since he didn't want to have to alter his life while he was still so young, he was already reaping the benefits of getting more rest.

At first, he'd felt that his diagnosis meant that he was going to have a different life from the one he'd always dreamed of having. He'd felt that a romantic relationship was no longer in the stars for him. After confessing that to his family, however, they'd urged him to keep his heart open to love anyway. They kept telling him that he was still a sweet, funny, hardworking guy and that any woman would be lucky to have him.

He had to admit to himself that, despite his diagnosis, he did feel as though he had something to give. There was a large part of him that still wanted to settle down and have a family of his own someday.

There was a soft knock on his office door, and a moment later his employee Keith stuck his head inside the room. "Hey, boss, that car is here for the brake replacement. Do you want to do that one, or—" Keith's voice got quieter, and he seemed to be taking in how exhausted Dean looked. "Or I can take care of it if you want."

Dean grimaced a little bit. Brake replacement was a difficult job, and it was ordinarily one that he liked to do himself, since the brakes were the most important safety feature on any car. Keith was a highly capable employee, however, and he trusted him to do the job well. "I hate to give you such a big task, but I'm just not up for it. Sorry, Keith. I know I'd said I wanted to do that car myself, but my body just isn't playing fair right now."

"Don't you worry about it." Keith shook his head. "I could use the extra money anyhow." He winked cheerfully and disappeared, and Dean smiled to himself, thinking about how lucky he was to have such a supportive, cooperative staff.

A moment later, however, his spirits dropped again. He suddenly felt overwhelmed by how quickly his life was changing. He never would have hesitated to take on a physically challenging task in the past, but now he felt as though if he tried to pick up a tool, his weak hands might drop it. He dropped his head into his hands, wondering what on earth he was going to do.

"Dean!"

He looked up, startled, to see his sister Alexis Bennett walking into the room. Her long reddish-brown hair was pulled back into a ponytail, and she was wearing jeans and a plain white blouse, which implied that she was on her way to work at the pub that night.

"Hey, Alexis, what's—"

She shook her head, coming to sit down on the edge of the desk near him. "You look exhausted. You're pale, and there are huge circles under your eyes. You've clearly been doing too much work all week. Go home and rest, please. There's no reason for you to be sitting in here. Go somewhere more comfortable."

Dean shook his head. "I'm fine, really. Yes, I'm a little tired, but I'm taking a break. I don't want to go home now, my shop closes in an hour. I can stick it out that long."

Alexis crossed her arms, and she got a look in her eyes that he knew meant business.

"Do your guys need you here in order to do their jobs correctly?"

"Well, no, but—"

"And are you the only person who can lock up for the night?"

"No, I'm not, but—"

"Dean." Alexis's tone was gentle. "You need to be realistic and accept the facts. This isn't the way to take care of yourself. There are ways to ensure that you still have a great quality of life—but being in denial and pushing yourself too hard too often are not two of those ways."

Dean took a deep breath and sighed. For a moment, he was at a loss for words. "Alexis, I don't know what else to do. This is what I do. I work. I'm a mechanic. I enjoy it, and I take pride in it. I want to live a normal life, and I have no intention of succumbing to aging way too soon because of this."

"I know." She reached over and squeezed his hand. "I understand how you feel, and I know how hard it is. I wish you didn't have to go through any of this, but I believe there's a way for you to still feel young and fulfilled, and also take care of yourself so that you don't feel like this."

"I hope you're right." He sighed, finding it difficult to keep his spirits up.

"This isn't the Dean I know. Being so tired is making you feel downhearted. You go home and rest. We're going to figure this out, but right now all you need to do is take care of yourself in this moment."

"Okay." He smiled weakly. "You're right. I should go home and rest."

She smiled back at him and stood up. "Make yourself some tea and a nice meal. Read a book or watch a movie. Do something you enjoy. You'll feel better in no time."

He stood up. "You want to walk out with me?"

"Well, I'm not staying here without you." She laughed.

"Let me just tell the guys that I'm going home and I'll be right back."

He popped into the garage to let his employees know that he was going home for the night. They seemed understanding and sympathetic, and even though he didn't want their pity, he felt grateful that they were so willing to stick with the work and close up the repair shop without him.

"Call me if you have any questions or something goes wrong." He drummed his fingers along the door frame, wishing he had the energy to stay.

"We will, but everything's going to go fine. These cars are in good hands. You get some rest, boss."

Dean smiled and went back into the office, where Alexis was standing by the door, texting someone with a dreamy smile on her face. Dean grinned when he saw her, guessing that the person that she was texting was her husband Grayson.

"You ready?" she asked him, looking up and smiling at him.

"Yeah, I'm ready." He repressed a sigh, still not wanting to leave his shop, but as he and Alexis stepped out into the late afternoon sunshine, he had to admit to himself that it might be nice to sit out on his porch for a while and read a book. It was a beautiful, cool afternoon, and there was a crisp scent in the air that heralded the coming of autumn.

The siblings began to stroll along the sidewalk together, and Dean noticed that Alexis was headed in the direction of The Lighthouse Grill, not her new house.

"Are you on your way to the pub?" he asked her.

"Yup." She chuckled. "It's just another day of scribbling down orders of tuna melts and bringing people sides of ranch."

He glanced at her, wondering if she was starting to get tired of waitressing. She was still smiling, but there had been a slight edge of frustration in her voice. "Are you not enjoying it anymore? I remember you'd said you loved working alongside our other family members as a waitress. You'd said it was just the spark of adrenaline you'd been missing back in L.A."

"Oh, I'm still enjoying it. I'm sure I always will, although I never would have thought that I'd be so content to be a waitress back when I was a model. It's a far cry from being on the cover of a Los Angeles fashion magazine, but it's been so invigorating to have real work to do. And I do love working with our family so much. It's just that sometimes being a waitress feels too repetitive. It's not that I mind the job, it's that I miss having a creative outlet. I want to be able to do something that involves my imagination. There's not much creativity involved in waitressing."

"Hey, have you ever tried rearranging people's food on their plates to make faces? I did that once in high school. Dad almost fired me."

Alexis threw her head back, laughing. "You did, huh? No, I haven't tried that, and I don't think making faces out of food would be enough to scratch my creative itch, anyway."

"Well, I bet you'll come up with something that will. You should ask that handsome hunk of a husband of yours. I know he's usually got his head in numbers, being a finance guy, but I'd wager that he could offer you some good advice."

"Hmm, that's a good idea." She got the dreamy smile on her face that she'd had when she was texting in Dean's office. "He's a pretty smart man."

"I'll say. He realized that his neglect of you was about to end your marriage, so he sold his extremely lucrative finance company and moved out here to be with you in a grand gesture. Most people aren't that smart. Most people would have chosen money over happiness."

She grinned. "He is smart. And it's not like we're without money, either—that new financial consultant job of his pays great. Not as much as before, obviously, but who needs to be that rich?"

He smiled at his sister. "You're smart too. You had a big mansion and all the money you could want, and you'd rather be here with your family."

"Hey, you guys are much better than a bunch of big empty rooms."

They gave each other a sideways hug, and Dean felt another surge of gratitude that she was back home again.

"Well, I'm really glad you're happy, Alexis. I really am."

"Thank you. I never could have imagined things would end up like this right after Dad died. I was so sure I was going to lose Grayson. But now things are going great with us, and I'm so grateful to have my husband back again." They walked quietly for another few moments, and then she bumped her shoulder against his playfully. "You're next. We're going to find you a woman."

He grimaced good-naturedly. "We'll see. I'm

starting to wonder if I'm just destined to never find love."

She shook her head firmly. "Every single woman in this town considers you to be a dreamboat. It was the same way in high school, and it's still true."

"Oh, it is, huh? And how do you know this?"

Her eyes danced gleefully. "I have my methods."

He chuckled and knocked his shoulder against hers in return. "Okay, Madam Matchmaker."

They gave each other a hug at the corner and she started to make her way to the pub, calling to him to make sure to get good rest.

"I will!" He waved as she disappeared around another corner. He started walking again, moving slowly as he made his way back home. He thought to himself that although he was apparently considered a catch by the single ladies of Rosewood Beach, he still didn't feel confident that he would ever find love. He'd never found a girl that he felt he'd like to spend the rest of his life with, and now that his diagnosis was part of his reality, love seemed out of the question sometimes. He didn't know how on earth he would be able to add a relationship to his life when he was already struggling just to work and spend time with his family without getting exhausted.

He reached his house and smiled quietly to

himself. Resting sounded great to him, now that he'd arrived home. He decided he would drink a glass of apple juice and read a mystery book while sitting out on his porch. Then all at once he found himself wishing that he had someone to come home to, not just an empty house.

*We'll see what happens,* he thought as he began to unlock his front door. *I hope Alexis is right. Having someone to love could be wonderful.*

Noelle Calhoun smiled as she closed the cover of her planner. She tucked the pink pen that she'd been using into her pen holder, which was silver and shaped like a little owl. She glanced around her office, thinking to herself that she should go around to some rummage sales that weekend and try to find more charming paintings and photographs to hang on the walls.

She'd moved to Rosewood Beach recently, and she was still settling into her new physical therapy office. She'd decorated it in pastel colors, which she found calming and uplifting at the same time. Her desk was organized but a little messy at the moment, since she was a little behind in her work. She smiled as she looked at the photograph of her and her grandparents which was sitting next to her computer. She'd moved from Wisconsin to Rosewood Beach to be closer to them, since they'd lived in Rosewood Beach for years. She'd always loved her grandparents, and being able to spend more time with them than ever before felt incredibly rewarding.

She was enjoying her new busy schedule, but she was still adapting to it, and little tasks kept creeping up on her unexpectedly. Not only did she have a lot of new patients, but she was still moving into her new place. In addition to that, she was making a point of spending plenty of time with her grandparents, and she was also determined to learn how to cook better. When she'd lived in Wisconsin, she'd ordered takeout for a lot of her meals, but now that she was in a little town that sold delicious local produce and had a wide variety of affordable items at the grocery store, she was determined to learn how to cook the kind of fancy, creative meals she'd always wanted to.

*Besides*, she thought, grinning to herself, *there's just something about this town that makes me want to be healthy and productive like that. People here make it look so easy to take care of yourself.*

When she'd first moved to Rosewood Beach, she hadn't been sure that she would like living in such a small town, but now that she was settling in, she was enjoying being there very much.

She leaned toward the bouquet of flowers that was resting on the edge of her desk and took a long sniff. She smiled cheerfully, thinking to herself that buying the bouquet from the general store that morning had most definitely been the right choice. She'd wanted a little something extra to brighten up her office, and the bouquet of daisies and chrysanthemums was just doing the trick. She thought about how the bouquet was just one of many nice things that had come her way since moving to Rosewood Beach. So far, she'd found a wonderful old book at the library, a lavender lemon doughnut at Seaside Sweets Bakery that was her new favorite dessert, a quiet spot overlooking the ocean in one of the town's parks, and now this beautiful bouquet of flowers.

*I have a feeling that I'm really going to like it here in Rosewood Beach,* she thought. *It's a welcoming place in so many ways.*

As if to prove her thought, at that moment her fellow physical therapist, Chip, knocked on the door of her office.

"Hey." Chip stuck his head inside the door and grinned at her. "You're done for the day, right? No more appointments?"

"Nope, I just finished my last one," she said. She grinned back. "Why? Are you done too?"

"Yup, I've been done for an hour. I've just been sitting around catching up on paperwork. What do you say to going to get some of the best hamburgers in town?"

"Sounds incredible." Her stomach growled at the thought, and she chuckled. "Where do we find these fabled best hamburgers?"

"At The Lighthouse Grill."

"Oh, sounds charming."

"It is. It's been family-run for decades. It's probably the most popular place in town."

"Well, no wonder, with those hamburgers." She stood up and grabbed her purse off a coat rack before turning to Chip. "Let's go. I'd love to."

"Perfect. Let me close up my office quick, and I'll meet you in the lobby in two minutes."

Chip disappeared, and she took a few moments to tidy up her desk a little. She thought about how kind Chip had been ever since she'd arrived to share the physical therapy practice with him. He was a good-natured, professional colleague, and already a good friend.

So far, she hadn't met too many other people in town, but she knew that gradually, she would get to know more and more of the people of Rosewood Beach. She smiled to herself before leaving the office, wondering what interesting people she was going to meet in the coming months and years.

# CHAPTER TWO

Julia Owens parked her car on the street outside the house of her boyfriend, Cooper Harris, and smiled. She'd parked there so many times, it was beginning to feel as though the road was developing grooves for her car's wheels.

It was a crisp, sunny Saturday morning, and she took a deep breath of the pleasant-smelling air as she stepped out of her car. She was so looking forward to fall, and all of the different delights that always accompanied it. She was looking forward to this fall in particular, because now she had Cooper and Macey to share it with.

Her stomach grumbled, and she thought eagerly about the breakfast that she was going to get with

Cooper that morning. She glanced at her watch as she walked up to the house. She wanted to make sure she had enough time to show Macey the snacks that she'd made for her before she and Cooper dropped the little girl off at daycare. She looked down at the tote bag she was carrying, feeling proud of what she'd made. She'd done research on some of the best homemade snacks for toddlers, since she wanted to give Macey special care. She'd made cinnamon apple chips, sliced pears spread with ricotta cheese, and yogurt bites, and although she'd been surprised by how time-consuming making the snacks had been, she liked the idea of giving Macey healthy snacks. Besides, she'd nibbled some of the snacks herself while making them and she'd found them to be delicious as well as fun to create.

Next to the snacks, in the tote bag there was also a little baby doll. She'd seen it at the Rosewood Beach toy store a few days earlier, when she'd been window shopping with Hazel and Dean. She'd immediately thought of Macey and had decided to surprise the little girl with the doll right away, rather than wait for her birthday or Christmas to roll around.

When she'd first met Cooper—after he'd saved

her from falling into a puddle by catching her in the rain—she had been unsure about how she would handle helping care for the little girl. She'd never expected to be dating a man with a child. She'd never spent much time with little children, and she didn't know if it would be beyond her scope or not. But the more time she'd spent with Macey, the more she'd come to adore the little girl. Now, she always looked forward to seeing her almost as much as she looked forward to seeing Cooper. Her relationship with the two of them was, besides her relationships with her family members, one of the best things in her life. Cooper was always supportive of her, encouraging her new favorite hobby of cooking, and cheering her on when she had to work long hours handling the financial side of her family's restaurant, The Lighthouse Grill.

Before she got a chance to ring the doorbell, the door was tugged open by Cooper, who immediately greeted her with a grin and a big hug.

"Hey, sweetheart." He kissed the side of her head affectionately. "Good morning."

"Good morning." She grinned at him, and then felt Macey's chubby little arms wrap themselves around her legs. "Good morning, sunshine!" She reached down and lifted the little girl up into her arms to give her a proper hug. "I have some presents for you."

"Presents!" Macey squealed. "Thank you!"

"Good job, Macey." Cooper gave his daughter a high-five, praising the way she'd said "thank you" without being prompted.

Julia reached into her tote bag and pulled out a bag of cinnamon apple chips and two Tupperwares filled with yogurt bites and the pears spread with ricotta cheese.

"I made you these yummy snacks. And they're healthy." She winked at Cooper. "There are some yogurt bites, some apple chips, and some pears spread with ricotta cheese. And I put snacks for you to take to daycare today into this little tin with the fairies on it. There's a couple of yogurt bites and some pear slices in there."

"Thank you, Julia." Cooper gave her a sideways hug, smiling at the way his daughter seemed thrilled by the snacks. "Those sound great."

"Here's this tin for her to take today, and I can go put the rest of the snacks in the refrigerator." She started toward the kitchen but stopped when Cooper handed her back the tin.

"Go ahead and put that in the fridge too. I'm sorry, sweetheart, but I think those snacks sound a little too messy for daycare. But I'll give them to her later. Besides, I already packed her bag for daycare last night."

"Oh, sure." Julia felt a slight flutter of disappointment, but she took it in stride. She reminded herself that her affection for Macey didn't make her a child expert, and there were still a lot of things she was learning.

"Well." She grinned at the little girl. "I have something else for you too." She reached inside her bag and then presented the baby doll. "Ta da!"

Macey gasped and reached for the doll. She held it tightly for a few moments, and then Cooper gently picked it up.

"Look, Macey." He crouched down to be on her level. "She's got a pretty little bonnet with this flower on it, and these beautiful silver buttons on her dress. Wow. What do we say to Julia?"

"Thank you!" Macey gave Julia another hug.

"You're so welcome." Julia drew in a breath, feeling her heart warm to see the toddler look so happy.

Cooper stood up and tucked the doll onto the top shelf of the closet. Julia watched him in surprise.

"I was thinking she could take that to daycare," Julia said, feeling disappointed again.

Cooper shook his head. "Sorry." He grimaced sympathetically. "That doll is an antique, and it's more for decoration than a toy. Or maybe for an older child, but I'm worried those antique buttons could cut her. They're so thin. And the doll is made of porcelain, so if she drops it and it breaks, then she really could get cut."

"Oh." Julia felt deflated. "I'm sorry, I—"

"Don't be sorry." He pulled her toward him and gave her a quick kiss. "You're being so sweet, and Macey and I both appreciate it so much. We'll give her that doll when she's a bit older. That should be perfect."

She bit her lip, wanting to tell him that she'd done her research and found out that the doll was supposed to be two-year-old friendly. It was a new toy and was probably made to look like an antique doll without actually being one. After a moment, however, she decided that it was best not to argue about what he thought was best.

"Come on, Macey, are you ready to go see your friends?" Cooper asked, smiling at the little girl.

"Yeah!" Thankfully, Macey seemed to have

forgotten all about the doll. Cooper picked up her daycare bag and took her hand.

"You go get her settled into the car, and I'll drop these snacks off in the fridge," Julia said, smiling.

"Sounds good. See you in a couple of minutes." He blew a kiss at her and stepped out through the front door.

Julia hurried into the kitchen, where she carefully tucked the snacks inside the refrigerator. She sighed as she placed the little tin on the top of the Tupperware stack. She didn't think that pears and ricotta cheese would be too messy for daycare, but she reminded herself that Macey would enjoy the snacks at home.

*And at least I've become more of an expert in child snacks,* she thought with a chuckle as she made her way back to the front door. *I've got some recipes under my belt, and I know what kinds of snacks Cooper doesn't want Macey to bring to daycare.*

She locked the front door behind her and made her way to Cooper's car, where he was just getting Macey settled into her car seat.

"You need some water, Macey?" Julia asked as she and Cooper sat down in the front seats of the car.

"I just gave her some orange juice before we left." Cooper smiled at her as he started the engine, and the sound of a kiddie songs CD suddenly filled the air.

"Oh, sure." Julia smiled. "You're always on top of things like that."

He reached over and squeezed her hand as a way of thanking her for the compliment. "I've had to do everything on my own for a while now. I was always nervous I wasn't doing enough, so I've tried my best to be on top of everything." He laughed.

She shook her head, squeezing his hand back. "You're a great father. I don't know why you ever worried."

"Well, she can really be a handful sometimes." Cooper grinned at Macey through the rearview mirror. "Can't you, kiddo?"

Macey offered him a pleased, chubby smile, and Julia and Cooper laughed.

A few minutes later, they arrived at the brightly colored daycare. Cooper parked the car, and Julia got out, intending to get Macey out of her car seat. By the time she reached the other side of the car, however, Cooper had already done so.

They walked inside the daycare together, and Macey looked excited. Julia saw a little table where a bunch of toddlers were sitting, scribbling happily on a large sheet of paper with crayons.

"Look, Macey, maybe you can color—" Julia started to say, but when she turned around, Cooper had already led his daughter over to a little reading nook where one of the teachers was getting ready to read a story out loud.

Once Macey had settled down happily on a bean bag chair next to the other kids, Cooper turned to Julia with a smile. "Are you ready to go get breakfast?"

"Let me say 'bye to Macey quick before we go," she said, taking a step forward.

Cooper shook his head. "It's best to just slip away quietly while she's distracted with something else. She knows we're coming back for her. This way she won't cry or make a fuss."

Julia pressed her lips together and nodded. "Okay. Let's go then." She'd wanted to say goodbye to Macey, but she understood the logic behind what Cooper was saying. After all, he had a lot more experience in dropping his daughter off at daycare than she did.

They made their way out of the building, both of them looking over their shoulders as they went to make sure that Macey was still happy and occupied. Once they'd stepped back out into the sunlight, Cooper took Julia's hand.

"What do you think? Pancakes or waffles? Or a skillet?"

"Oh, gosh, I don't know. They all sound amazing." She smiled at him, but inside she was feeling disappointed. She couldn't help feeling that he didn't need her help at all with his daughter, who she had come to love with all her heart.

# CHAPTER THREE

Hazel listened to the sound of her sisters laughing and smiled. She was tucked up comfortably in a corner of her mother's cozy couch, listening to Julia and Alexis laugh about a mishap that had occurred at The Lighthouse Grill earlier that day. She lifted her wine glass to her lips and took a slow sip, reflecting on how grateful she felt to be there.

*My siblings always lift my spirits*, she thought. *I'm so glad I didn't turn down this opportunity to spend time with them.*

She'd only considered declining Julia's invitation for a moment, since she almost always accepted an opportunity to spend time with her siblings. She'd felt a bit down and listless earlier in the afternoon, since she'd seen the local handyman Jacob Dorsey at the grocery store, and she'd realized that she had just as much of a crush on him as ever, even though she'd kept telling herself that she'd fully accepted the reality that he had a girlfriend now and was now off-limits. She'd been doing her best to keep her spirits up ever since her plans to ask him out had been unexpectedly dashed by learning that he was dating someone else, but it was hard sometimes.

"You remember her, don't you, Hazel?" Julia turned toward her with a smile, shattering her reverie. "Mrs. Henderson?"

Hazel grinned. "The sweet old lady who always puts fresh flowers in her hat?"

"Yes!" Julia gesticulated wildly. "And we're all watching from the windows as this young man is following her around, trying to shoo away the bee that's having a grand old time of it on her hat."

Hazel laughed at the story, but in the next moment her heart gave a slight pang as she thought about how Jacob was the kind of person who would do something like that. He was always kind and helpful—he'd been so kind and helpful to her that she'd gotten her hopes up that he liked her in the same way that she liked him.

"Oh, that's too funny." Alexis was almost shaking with laughter as she reached for her apple galette.

After she took a bite, she said, "I love being here with you two. There's nothing better than having fun chatting with my sisters like this."

Hazel beamed at her sister, and Julia said, "Aww! I feel the same way."

The sisters had settled down together in the living room to drink red wine and eat apple galettes after a delicious dinner of chicken alfredo lasagna. Julia had invited all her siblings earlier in the day, since Vivian was away visiting a friend for the night and Julia had expressed a desire for company.

"Are you sure, though?" Hazel cocked a brow as she picked up her galette, getting ready to take a bite. "Is there nothing better than chatting with us? Not even spending time with your husband?"

Alexis flushed and smiled, her eyes immediately taking on a starry look. Hazel and Julia glanced at each other and grinned.

"I mean, I guess if we're talking literally—" Alexis laughed. "There is something special about spending time with Grayson that nothing else can compare to."

"I'm so glad that your marriage is being rekindled," Julia said, reaching over to Alexis and giving her a sideways hug. "Grayson is a lucky guy. I'm glad you gave him a second chance."

"Well, he's really been earning it." Alexis smiled dreaming down into her wine glass. "He's been doing all kinds of sweet things, like buying me flowers or leaving love notes on the bathroom mirror in the morning. If you'd told me he'd be acting like this a year ago, I would never have believed it." She stared into space for a moment, looking incredibly happy. "But I think the thing I love the most about the way he's changed is how much time we spend together. We eat breakfast together in the morning, and dinner together almost every night. We sit and talk together, and I get to look into his eyes during our conversations. It's wonderful."

"Sounds fantastic." Hazel smiled at her sister, wondering if she would ever be lucky enough to find a love like that.

"Thank you, Hazel. It really is. I'm so happy to have the man I married back."

For a few moments, the sisters sat in silence, all smiling quietly. Hazel took another bite of her galette, savoring the sweet, tangy flavor of the filling and the buttery crust.

"I love your nails, Hazel," Julia said after a moment, looking with fascination at Hazel's hands. "Are those little flower images?"

Hazel laughed, looking down at her nails and

feeling pleased. "Yes, these are some water transfer designs that I saw online. They're cute, aren't they? Except I did them yesterday and they're already chipping. Oh well." She heaved a pretend sigh and grinned. "I'd just wanted to do a little something to have a bit of a glow up. I mean, a woman doesn't have to have a boyfriend in order to want to look nice, right?"

"Oh, definitely not!" Julia nodded emphatically.

"Of course you don't need a boyfriend for all that stuff." Alexis sat down next to Hazel and gave her a hug. "You should always do what makes you feel beautiful, just for fun. As a treat to yourself."

"I completely agree." Julia grinned. "I mean, I was single for years and years, and I always got manicures." She held up her fingers, which were manicured a beautiful dark red.

"Besides, what happened with Jacob has nothing to do with you." Alexis squeezed Hazel's knee. "You're just as worthy of care and attention as you always were. Just because he missed the boat doesn't mean that you shouldn't pamper yourself."

Hazel sighed. "He's not the one who missed the boat; I am. I wish I'd had the courage to ask him out sooner. Maybe then he'd be dating me instead of this other girl."

Alexis shook her head. "Don't think like that. You couldn't have known. Besides, who knows what's going to happen next? You might meet some amazing man who will totally sweep you off your feet. And in the meantime, you paint your nails to your heart's content."

Hazel smiled, feeling grateful for her sisters' support. "I don't know that I want a man, really. I mean, Jacob is Jacob..." She found herself growing sad suddenly, and she shook her head, trying to dispel those thoughts. "I just mean, I don't know that having a boyfriend in general is really my goal. I want to pick myself back up after this disappointment and feel like myself again. I've done just fine raising Samantha without a man for many years, and I'm going to keep right on doing it."

"That's the spirit!" Julia gave a satisfied nod. "I am hoping you do find love, Hazel, at least someday, but you certainly don't need a man. You've created an amazing life for yourself and your daughter, and you have every reason to be content without a boyfriend. And besides," she added, arching a brow, "if Dean were here, he would remind us that men hardly ever notice women's glow ups anyway, not unless they're completely drastic like a whole new hair color. So what's the point in doing it for men, anyway? We should just do it for ourselves!"

Alexis and Hazel laughed. Hazel thought about how many times she'd done little things to try to get various men's attention over the years, almost none of which had been noticed. Her sisters and friends, however, had always noticed those little details right away.

"Oh, Dean." Alexis shook her head, smiling. "I think if one of these girls in town who's attracted to him dyed her hair blue, he still wouldn't notice. He's so oblivious when it comes to women being interested in him." She chuckled. "I guess a lot of guys are like that."

"I miss Dean." Hazel sighed, hugging her knees. She wasn't used to her twin not being at every family get-together. In the past, they'd been almost inseparable. She knew things were tough for him because of his osteoarthritis, and she didn't blame him for turning down Julia's invitation, but she wished that things were different and that he had the energy to be there with them that night. "It's so hard to see him struggling with his energy like this. I wish there was something we could do."

"I know." Alexis leaned her head against the couch cushions, biting her lip.

"Well, maybe there is." Julia pulled her phone out of her pocket and began to click away on it. "I've been doing research on things that could help Dean. And I found this." She held her phone out to her sisters, revealing an article on a medical website. "This outlines the benefits of physical therapy for osteoarthritis."

Alexis and Hazel leaned forward in interest.

"Physical therapy?" Alexis echoed.

Julia nodded. "I was doing research this morning during some down time at the pub. I found a bunch of articles on how physical therapy can improve strength and flexibility and reduce pain in patients with osteoarthritis."

"Oh, that's great!" Hazel clasped her hands, feeling a surge of excitement. "That should help him."

"Yeah, but what if he's stubborn and doesn't want to do it?" Alexis sipped her wine thoughtfully.

"We'll just have to convince him to do it," Julia said, nodding her head firmly. "He shouldn't pass up a chance to feel better like this."

"I'll threaten to never bake him cookies again if he doesn't do it." Hazel laughed. "He should do it, though, really. Why pass up an opportunity to make his life better?"

Julia grinned. "I bet we can convince him."

Soon, the sisters started a game of cards, playing on the coffee table while they continued to drink their wine and munch their galettes. Hazel found herself feeling introspective as they played, and she thought about how much she hoped that Dean would go to physical therapy and improve his quality of life.

*Everyone needs to do something for themselves to live their best life*, she thought. *For me, right now that's just a bit of self-care to remind myself that being a strong, independent woman is wonderful. For Dean, it's taking on this new challenge that will make him feel better.*

She smiled as she laid down a card, feeling suddenly hopeful and optimistic. She had a feeling that things were about to get better for both her and her twin.

# CHAPTER FOUR

Dean strolled down the sidewalk toward Seaside Sweets Bakery, with his hands in his pockets. It was a beautiful sunny morning, and there was a slight chill in the air which made the world feel fresh. He whistled quietly to himself, thinking how glad he was that he felt a bit better that morning. He had no pain, and he felt significantly more rested than usual.

*Too bad I had to go to sleep at eight p.m. to feel this way,* he thought, chuckling wryly to himself. *It's far from ideal. But at least it worked.*

He reached the bakery and stepped inside. It was warm in the cozy little shop, and the air smelled fragrant with the sweet aroma of baked goods. Dean went up to the counter and ordered a bear claw and a cup of coffee. He'd just received his purchases and was about to leave the shop when the front door opened and all three of his sisters spilled inside.

"There!" Hazel said triumphantly. "I told you guys he went in here."

Dean laughed, opening his arms for a group hug. "What is this, an intervention?"

"It is, in a way." Julia had a determined look on her face, and he knew that whatever his sisters were about to say to him, they really meant business. "Come on and sit down with us."

Dean glanced at his watch. "Well, I don't really have time right now. I'm supposed to be at the auto shop in fifteen minutes. If I stay to talk now, I'm going to be late."

Alexis shook her head. "Your employees will understand. This is important."

"Uh, okay." Dean could see that there would be no denying his sisters. He wondered what on earth could be so important to discuss right at that moment that they were insisting he arrive late to his shop. "What did you want to talk with me about?"

Hazel took him by the arm and his sisters led him over to one of the tables that was placed by a window. It was a fairly secluded spot, tucked partly behind a display of homemade knit hats and socks.

"This is a good table," Alexis said, looking around with a pleased expression once they'd sat down. "It's fairly private."

"What is going on?" Dean asked, leaning forward to add emphasis to his words. "Why do we need to talk somewhere private? This isn't about a girl, is it?"

Julia laughed. "No, it's not about a girl."

"But we can get to that later." Alexis waggled her brows mischievously. "There are still plenty of eligible single women in this town you haven't let me try to matchmake you with yet."

"I'm good, thanks." Dean shook his head, laughing. "We can discuss my romantic prospects another day, if you don't mind. What's all this hullabaloo about?"

"We did some research," Julia said, clicking on her phone and sliding it across the table toward him. On the screen was an article about physical therapy. "And we learned that going to physical therapy could greatly improve your symptoms. It could majorly improve your quality of life."

He watched her face, seeing how excited she was, and feeling a sinking sensation in his chest. He glanced down at the article, noting that it was from a reputable medical journal.

"It could be so good for you." Hazel reached across the table and squeezed his hand. "It says in that article that it could improve your pain and increase strength."

"If it goes well, you'll be able to do more because you'll feel better." Alexis smiled at him, and he could see in her eyes that she had just as much hope in the plan as his other two sisters did.

He was touched by how much they cared about him, but he couldn't get rid of an almost overpowering feeling of reluctance.

"Come on," Julia urged him. "What are you thinking? Will you do it?"

Dean sighed. "I appreciate you three wanting to take care of me and do what's best for me. Really, I do. But I'm feeling good today. I really don't see a need for me to go to physical therapy."

He didn't want to say it out loud, but the thought of going to physical therapy made him feel nearly as decrepit as his osteoarthritis diagnosis had in the first place. He associated physical therapy with having debilitating conditions or injuries. He didn't think that someone like him—who was still generally very functional—needed to go to physical therapy. After all, if it was exercise that was supposed to be good for him, he was already getting plenty of that in the repair shop by walking around and lifting heavy objects regularly.

"That's today." Hazel shook her head, looking determined. "You may not feel like this tomorrow. We've all seen you get exhausted. We know you're struggling to balance work and family life with your fatigue. This could really help."

"Yes!" Alexis nodded in agreement. "I mean, you had to miss our get-together last night because you were feeling too tired. Didn't you say you were going to go to sleep around eight or something?"

Dean nodded. "Yeah. I did. I was in bed by seven thirty and asleep by eight."

"Don't you see?" Julia shook her head. "I'm glad that worked for you and you feel good today, but you shouldn't have to turn down evening plans and go to bed by eight every night in order to feel good the next day. Physical therapy can help you. Wouldn't you rather go to physical therapy than have to go to bed super early every single night?"

Dean sighed. They'd found the hole in his argument almost right away.

"I hear what you're saying, but we don't know that physical therapy is going to work. It might not. Maybe just actually resting more often is the only thing that will really work for me."

"But it might work!" Hazel tapped her fingers on the table enthusiastically. "It might make you feel amazingly better. Why don't you just try it for a few sessions and then you can decide? If it makes you feel better, great! You've found a workable solution to your condition. If it doesn't work, then you don't need to do it anymore."

"Okay." Dean smiled. "You've got me there. That's a good idea. I'll try it, I guess."

"Come on, try to contain your enthusiasm," Julia teased. "You're acting like we've just convinced you to take a polar plunge or something. It won't be that bad. I bet you'll end up loving it. Besides, I already did some research on where you could go for physical therapy, and it turns out that there's a new PT in town who has a really impressive resume."

Dean shrugged. "I mean, that's great, but I don't care about whether or not the person has great training or experience. I'll just show up and do it and see if it helps."

"And it will, and you'll be thanking us profusely in a few weeks," Hazel said cheerfully.

He shook his head, chuckling. "I guess we'll have to wait and see."

*I'll appease my sisters by going to a few sessions and be done with it,* he thought. *It can't be that bad, and if I don't try it, I know they won't let me hear the end of it.*

He noticed the time on a clock that was hanging on the wall behind Julia's head. "I should get to the repair shop," he said, standing up. "Thanks for coming up with all this, you guys. I appreciate you caring about me like this."

"Of course." Julia gave him a hug. "I bet this will help turn your life around."

"We'll see," he said doubtfully, starting toward the door. He noticed in a moment that they weren't following him. "Are you guys coming back out?"

"As long as we're here, I think we're going to get some pastries and coffee," Hazel said, glancing cheerfully at the display case packed with delicious items.

"Oh, and talk amongst yourselves about how silly your brother Dean is being and how he's going to see how right you are very soon?" He laughed.

"Of course!" Alexis grinned at him. "Have a good day at the shop."

He laughed more, shaking his head, as he waved goodbye to his sisters and stepped back out into the sunlight. As he made his way to the repair shop, he found himself wondering what physical therapy might be like. He still felt reluctant to try it and doubtful that it would work out well for him, but he had to admit that finding some kind of solution for his diagnosis was a pleasant idea. If something could help him with his symptoms, that would be a wonderful turn of events.

# CHAPTER FIVE

Alexis hummed quietly to herself as she tidied up her kitchen. Afternoon sunlight was streaming across the wooden floorboards and the countertops, and gleaming on the dishes that she was tucking inside the cupboards. Through the window above the sink she could see the backyard, where the first signs of autumn were already beginning to appear. There was a faint yellow flush to the leaves of the trees, and the apples on the little apple tree were a rosy red.

She picked up the mug of coffee that she'd been slowly sipping since she got up that morning. She'd had a slow, relaxing start to her day. She'd read in bed for a little while before dressing and tidying up the house a little. She and Grayson had moved into their charming red brick Colonial house only recently, and she was still enamored with it. She was still getting used to all its little quirks, like the old milk door in the kitchen and the oddly-shaped cupboard underneath the stairs. It was a darling house, and she loved keeping it clean and organized. It smelled faintly of cedar, and her autumn-themed scented candles had been adding another layer of coziness to the scent of the house.

She glanced at the clock, noting that she would need to eat lunch soon and then leave. She was scheduled to work a shift at the pub that afternoon, and she was always careful to eat enough before working so that she had plenty of energy to sustain her through her shift. She knew she would need to eat quickly in order to get to work on time, and she decided to make herself a sandwich with cucumber slices and ranch on the side—something nutritional, but also quick and easy.

*I'll arrange those flowers first*, she thought, turning to the flowers she'd left on the edge of the counter that morning.

She knew that she needed to keep moving or she might be late for work, but she wanted to be sure to arrange the flowers before she left. She'd gone out into the garden that morning and picked most of the last remaining flowers. A frost was forecast for that evening, and she knew that the flowers wouldn't last outdoors overnight, so she'd decided to bring them inside where they would be well-appreciated and stay alive for a few days longer.

She picked out a beautiful red glass vase from the collection that she had stashed in one of the cupboards, and she filled it with water. As she began to arrange the flowers in the vase in a way that she found aesthetically pleasing, she thought about how nice it was to have her own home again. She'd loved staying with Hazel and Samantha, but there was something about owning her own space that was pleasant and soothing. She'd never had a home quite like this before, either—even though she and Grayson had shared a house in L.A., it had been a massive mansion and she'd never felt as though she could be truly comfortable in it. In addition to that, the fact that she and Grayson had grown into strangers when they were both still living in L.A. had taken away a great deal of the mansion's charm.

She began to hum again, and then sing quietly to herself. She was feeling contented and peaceful, and then all at once she let out a squeal as she felt someone hug her from behind. For a moment, all she felt was surprised, but in the next instant, she smelled Grayson's cologne and she grinned.

"Grayson!" She turned around, wiggling back into his arms for a front-facing hug. "What on earth are you doing home in the middle of the afternoon?"

"Surprised you, huh?" He grinned at her, and his light green eyes twinkled.

"Yes, very much." She hugged him tighter. "But I'm thrilled."

"I'm glad." He kissed her nose. "My last couple of meetings got rescheduled, so I picked up your favorite lunch from The Salty Spoon, and I figured that we could have a picnic outside together. Spend some time talking. Relaxing on this beautiful afternoon."

"Oh, I'd love to, but—" She turned around and glanced at the clock again. "I need to get to work soon. I was just going to throw together a quick sandwich and hurry off. I don't have time for a long picnic." Her stomach flopped in disappointment. "I so wish I could say yes. It's incredibly sweet of you."

"Well, I'd remembered that you'd said you were working this afternoon, so on my way home I stopped in and checked with Julia. She said that she would be happy to cover for you for as long as we want."

A radiant smile spread across Alexis's face. "Really? Oh, that's wonderful."

"You're welcome." He rocked her back and forth a little. "I've got meatloaf and mashed potatoes, and you've got chicken pot pie and a side of sweet potato fries. Word on the street is that it's your favorite meal there."

"It is." She felt touched not only that he'd surprised her with the picnic, but also that he had taken the time to figure out what her favorite meal at The Salty Spoon was. "Thank you, that's so sweet of you."

Her stomach growled loudly, and they both laughed.

"Come on," he said. "I've got the to-go containers in the car, and we can bring some dishes and a picnic blanket out to the backyard. I thought we could sit under the apple tree. It's always a good mixture of sunny and shady there."

As the two of them worked to set up their picnic, she reflected that she felt as though she was living in some kind of dream, having her husband back and acting so thoughtful. It felt extraordinary to spend time with him, since only a few months earlier he'd been so wrapped up in his work that he'd been completely ignoring her.

*My life is so beautiful*, she thought. *I'm so grateful. There's nothing missing anymore. I have a*

*job I love, and a husband I love. I get to spend time
with my family and create this home here.*

In the midst of her thoughts came a sudden
revelation—she did feel as though something was
missing. The realization startled her, and she didn't
understand it. As she laid out the picnic blanket with
Grayson, along with dishes for their takeout, she
pondered the idea. She could sense that what she felt
was missing she'd once had in L.A., but she didn't
know what that thing was. She knew she didn't want
to be a model anymore, and she didn't want to move
back to the city. Still, there was a part of her heart
that yearned for something she didn't have and she
felt as though she'd had it before, when she was
living out on the west coast.

*What is it?* she thought as she and Grayson sat
down to eat their meal on the picnic blanket. *There's
a little something missing from my life. Something
that L.A. fulfilled. But what? If only I could figure out
what it is.*

She felt a kind of restless yearning in her heart,
but she didn't know what she was yearning for. As
she and Grayson began to eat their meal, she
momentarily forgot her thoughts, distracted by how
delicious the food was and how affectionate her
husband was being. After a few minutes, however,

they fell to eating quietly in companionable silence, and the thoughts returned.

"Do you miss L.A.?" she asked him after a few more moments of pondering.

He looked up at her, surprised. "No, not at all. Are you worried that I'm not content with our life here?"

She shook her head hurriedly, not wanting him to think that she was worried. It was clear to her that he was very content with their new life, and she was as well—barring this little unidentified thing that she felt was missing.

"No, not at all, sweetheart. It's just—well, I was just curious. Life used to be so different for both of us, didn't it? In so many different ways. I'm just thinking about all the ways our life is different now."

He smiled at her. "I can understand that."

She didn't say it out loud to her husband, but she was trying to figure out what the different thing was that she wanted back again. Was it being surrounded by hustle and bustle all the time? That couldn't be it, she'd never enjoyed living like that. She found the steady, easy pace of Rosewood Beach calming and uplifting. Was it the glitz and glamour? That couldn't be it either, she'd be able to recognize a desire like that. Besides, she hadn't even been doing her hair and makeup as carefully as she used to, so clearly she wasn't missing being glamorous.

"You seem lost in thought." Grayson smiled at her as he adjusted his position on the picnic blanket. He was half lying down, and she grinned at him, enjoying seeing him look so relaxed. He'd spent so many years being stressed and overwhelmed, and it did her heart good to see him taking it easy.

"I am." She laughed. "Reminiscing, I guess. Although I agree with you that I would never want to go back to L.A." She didn't want to tell Grayson that she felt as though something was missing from her life, because he might take her yearning too seriously and worry that she was truly discontent. She was deeply content with her life, she knew that —but at the back of her mind there was an itching feeling, urging her to find something that was missing.

# CHAPTER SIX

Hazel laughed as her daughter Samantha eagerly picked up a box of fall-themed cookies. The two of them were in the Rosewood Beach General Store, grabbing some items after Hazel had picked up Samantha from school. Hazel always enjoyed shopping with Samantha, since what had become routine to her was still new and fascinating to her daughter. Samantha always got excited about the wide variety of items that were available at the general store, and Hazel often found herself catching some of her daughter's enthusiasm.

"Go ahead and put those in the cart. I think we could use some leaf-shaped, pumpkin-flavored cookies in our lives." Hazel chuckled.

"I'll say." Samantha cheerfully plopped the box

into the cart. "We should eat them tonight while we watch a movie. Something fall-themed."

"Sounds great to me." Hazel grinned and looked back down at her shopping list. "We also need laundry detergent and hand soap. We should look for that cucumber mint soap again, I really liked that."

"Oh, I guess so, but shouldn't we get something fall-themed? Like apple or pumpkin spice or something?"

"Wow, you're really into these fall scents and flavors, aren't you?"

"You've been alive for a long time. This is only my twelfth autumn, and I basically wasn't conscious for the first two. You know, too little to appreciate it. So it's kind of only my tenth autumn. So it's very important."

Hazel had to fight off a fit of laughter. "Oh, boy, I love you. Okay. Fall-themed soap it is."

"Yay! I love you too, Mom."

"You want to run and grab the soap, and I'll get the laundry detergent?"

"Sure." Samantha scampered off in the next moment, and Hazel made her way to the aisle that held the laundry detergent. She left the cart at the endcap, and then turned the corner, her eyes on the shelves.

She was looking so intently at the laundry detergents, trying to see if she could find a fall-themed scent for Samantha, that she didn't notice the person standing nearby, intently reading the label on a bottle of cleaning solution.

She did, however, notice that person when she bumped right into him.

"Oh, I'm so sorry—Jacob!" Her heart skipped a beat as she found herself blinking up at Jacob Dorsey, the man she'd nearly professed her attraction to.

"Oh, gosh, hey, Hazel." He grinned at her and held up the bottle of cleaning solution apologetically. "Sorry, I got totally wrapped up in this. Lost in the world of chemical ingredients."

She laughed breathlessly. "Sounds fascinating."

"Oh, it is. Very." He smiled down at her, looking just as friendly as always, and she found her heart doing somersaults. "And it turns out that this does have the ingredients I need, so I'd better get going. Nice to see you."

"Good to see you too." She managed to get the words out without sounding as though she was stammering, even though she felt as though her heart was beating a mile a minute.

He waved briefly, still smiling, and then

disappeared around the end of the aisle. She watched him go, feeling a knot form in her stomach.

*Jacob never did anything wrong,* she thought, holding back a sigh. *There's no reason for him to linger and talk to me now, and I shouldn't feel bad about it. Why can't I just let it go?*

"Hey, Mom!"

Hazel turned, glad to hear her daughter's voice, and as soon as she'd turned around, she burst into laughter. "What on earth are those?"

Samantha was standing at the end of the aisle, striking a dramatic pose and wearing bright yellow sunglasses with lenses shaped like hearts. The frames were covered in imitation diamonds, and they glinted fiercely.

"Don't you like my new sunglasses?" Samantha did a flamboyant twirl. "I think they make me look really elegant."

"Those are outrageous." Hazel laughed.

Samantha shook her head. "They are the fashion."

"They would make anyone look like a bumblebee," Hazel said, still chuckling.

"Are you saying I look like a bumblebee?" Samantha's jaw dropped as she pretended to be offended.

"Come look at yourself in this mirror," Hazel said, catching sight of a mirror that was on the wall near a display of baseball caps. "You will agree with me."

Laughing, Samantha followed her mother over to the mirror, and as soon as she saw her reflection, she doubled over with laughter.

"Oh, man, that's good." Samantha snorted, straightening up. "Here. You try them on."

She took off the sunglasses and handed them to her mother, who put them on with a grin.

"Yup." Hazel turned to her reflection and started laughing again. "I'm the Mama Bumblebee."

"You're right, they do make us look like bumblebees." Samantha took the sunglasses as her mother handed them back to her. "So, we're buying them, right?"

Hazel shook her head, laughing. "Maybe you can buy a pair with your allowance."

Samantha sighed. "I just spent my allowance on a book. Which, when I think about it, is probably a much better purchase than these sunglasses. Although I did want to show my friends so we could laugh."

"Hey, bring them in here." Hazel grinned at her daughter. "You can all try on a pair." The laugh had done her heart good, reminding her that she had so much to be thankful for. She might not have Jacob Dorsey as a boyfriend, but she'd gotten along fine without him for many years. She had a darling daughter that she adored, and a kind, supportive family. As she and Samantha continued to shop, her spirits continued to lift as she reminded herself how lucky she was. After a few minutes, Samantha darted off to look at lawn ornaments, and Hazel became more lost in thought as she began to walk through the store by herself.

She remembered the conversation that she'd had with her sisters about pampering herself as a show of self-love. She smiled as she got the idea to purchase a face mask for herself, and a moment later she steered the cart into the beauty supply aisle.

She picked out a green tea and honey face mask, feeling pleased with her selection. She liked the idea of treating herself to an at-home spa experience. Then she checked her list again and saw that she'd made all her purchases.

*Too bad my daughter has disappeared,* she thought with a chuckle. *It's time for us to go.*

"Samantha!" she called, not quite shouting since she didn't want to disturb the other customers.

Samantha didn't appear, but she decided to start

checking out anyway, knowing that Samatha would know to come look for her at the front of the store sooner rather than later.

She was greeted by the friendly cashier and began to unload her cart onto the conveyer belt. As she worked, she noticed a catalog in the magazine rack. It was titled, *How to Make Your Own DIY Spa Day*.

Hazel picked up the catalog with interest. A few flips through the glossy pages told her that it was something she wanted to purchase. She thought that having a "do-it-yourself" spa day was a wonderful idea.

"Hey, Mom!" Samantha sashayed up to her. "Ooh, that looks cool."

"It does, doesn't it? I think I'm going to buy it."

As Hazel placed the catalogue down onto the conveyer belt, she felt a surge of excitement. Having a spa day would be the perfect way to treat herself with love and care, and remind herself that she didn't need a man in her life to feel happy.

\* \* \*

Dean leaned against his kitchen counter, rubbing his hands gently. He was frowning and staring into space. Next to him on the stove, a pot of freshly-made spaghetti was starting to cool. He'd made it for his dinner, but now he was beginning to lose his appetite.

He'd had a good day at work, until the very end. For most of the day, he'd had good energy and almost no pain. Then in the late afternoon, his hands had begun to hurt. He'd brushed off his concerns and kept working, but by the time he was back at home and cooking dinner for himself, his hands were in a lot of pain.

*And it's only the start of the week,* he thought. *I rested all weekend.*

Feeling a twist of worry, he turned around and got a plate out of the cupboard, along with a fork. He dished himself out a generous portion of spaghetti and meatballs, and then covered the pasta with a sprinkling of parmesan cheese. Then he plopped some pre-washed spinach leaves onto the side of his plate and drizzled ranch dressing over them, making a lazy salad. Finally, he sat down at his table with the plate of food and a can of lemon seltzer water.

He began to eat, relishing the taste of the food but unable to ignore the way his hands still ached with a dull pain. He tried to stay optimistic as he ate his meal, but he was becoming more and more worried.

He thought about what he might be able to do to help with the pain, and his mind lighted on the idea of compression. He paused in his eating for a moment, considering it. He wasn't sure if it would work or not, but he decided it was worth a try. He remembered that he had a wrist brace from when he'd tweaked his wrist playing baseball in high school. He wasn't exactly sure where it was, but he guessed that it was in an old box filled with high school paraphernalia that he kept up in the attic.

When he'd finished his meal, he felt refreshed and a little more energized. He went up to the attic and located the old box, and then he brought it back downstairs to the living room so he could look through it more comfortably.

He took a long sip of his seltzer water and began to dig into the box. The first thing he pulled out was his old baseball jersey, and he grinned when he saw it, immediately flooded with memories.

Below the jersey was a messy collection of items, including his high school yearbooks. He drew out the first one almost reverently, surprised by how intensely nostalgic he felt all of a sudden. He began to turn the pages slowly, a huge smile on his face as he relived old times in his mind.

He felt delighted by the pictures that he saw. He grinned as he saw old photographs of his classmates, marveling at how young everyone looked. He laughed over the sight of Hazel wearing braces, and a picture of himself with a black eye that he'd gotten playing baseball.

When he'd finished going through the yearbooks, he found a photo album underneath them. He remembered with a grin when Julia had given it to him, and he opened it eagerly. Inside were more pictures of his high school glory days—baseball games and board game nights with his friends—and then the pictures began to be of his first few years after high school, when he'd become a mechanic and worked at the local hardware store part time.

As he kept turning the pages, he began to see pictures from when he started his auto repair shop. There were photographs of the grand opening, and the party that they'd had in the garage afterward. He chuckled over pictures of the car-shaped cake that his mother had made, and the banner that Hazel had made that had read, "Congrats on the Best Auto Shop in Town."

His heart felt warmed by the sight of so many

good memories. He remembered how much energy and hope for the future he'd had.

*I want to prolong my youth*, he thought, feeling a sudden surge of determination. *I want to feel good like that again. If there's a way for that to happen, I'm going to take it.*

He closed the photo album, deciding that he was going to make a physical therapy appointment the following day.

# CHAPTER SEVEN

"Bye, Mr. Dawson! Great work today!"

Noelle stood in the lobby of the physical therapy clinic, waving to the sweet old man who was walking out the front door, carefully using his cane. He lifted a hand and waved back cheerfully, a huge smile on his face. She grinned at him, thinking to herself that he had probably been her favorite patient so far. He'd been incredibly sweet and good natured throughout his entire appointment, cracking silly jokes and laughing instead of complaining when he was struggling with something. He'd worn a button-down sweater with a dandelion tucked into one of the buttonholes, and when she'd asked him about it, he'd said, "I don't think dandelions get enough credit, do they? Look at how pretty it is."

"Oh, he's darling," she murmured as the door closed behind him. "What a sweetheart."

She turned around and started to head back toward her office, reflecting that her appointment with the elderly man had been a wonderful way to start her morning. Mr. Dawson had been her first and only patient so far that day, and he'd brightened her whole morning as completely as if it was his job.

*I love working with the older folks*, she thought as she stepped back inside her cozy office. *And in a small town like this, most of my patients are probably going to be on the elderly side.*

She smiled, sitting down at her desk and turning on her laptop. She was used to having a wide variety of patients, some of them healing from serious injuries and some of them struggling with conditions that made mobility difficult for them. She thought to herself that she might miss the challenges that came along with helping some of those kinds of patients, but she reminded herself that her work was always rewarding. It was a joy for her to see her patients improve their health and mobility, no matter what their struggles were.

She found herself staring into space, remembering how she always used to imagine that she might meet some handsome man who came to her as a therapy patient one day. She chuckled, shaking her head at the idea.

*I don't think that's likely to happen here,* she thought with a grin. *And that's fine with me. I've dated plenty. I could go for having some quiet in my life.*

She'd dated a fair amount of people over the years, although she'd never seemed to find that spark that made her want to settle down with someone permanently. It had all worked out for her in the long run, since her singleness had allowed her to move to a new town easily, and she was glad that she was there in Rosewood Beach. She had plenty of time to focus on her career and enjoy living quietly and peacefully.

In the next moment, there was a soft knock on her office door.

"Noelle? Your next patient is here."

The receptionist opened the door to Noelle's office a little and poked her head inside, smiling. Noelle glanced with surprise at her schedule, which she'd pulled up on her computer screen. She hadn't been expecting this patient, which meant that they had signed up for an appointment very recently.

"Send him in," she said breezily, glancing at the

appointment information on the screen and seeing that the patient's name was Dean Owens.

A young man stepped into her office. She was immediately taken aback by the fact that he was so young—close to her own age. It seemed like a strange coincidence that she'd just been thinking to herself that she was unlikely to have any young patients, and then she got one within minutes. He was handsome too, she thought, and looked pleasant. She liked the way his dark brown hair was a little messy, since it implied he was a laid-back person.

"Hello, Dean. I'm Noelle," she said, standing and offering her hand for a handshake. "Nice to meet you."

"Nice to meet you," he said, grasping her hand firmly and shaking it. She got the impression that he was a little uncomfortable, and she made a mental note to try to help him feel more at ease.

"So, Dean, what's going to happen first is I'll go over some questions with you. All general procedure. We'll go over things like your medical history, and you can tell me what your goals for physical therapy are. Sound good?"

"Sure." He nodded. "Sounds good." He spoke politely, but she got the sense that he was in a hurry to get things underway so that he could get out of there that much sooner.

"My first question is very important." She paused for dramatic effect, and then said, "What's your favorite color?"

His eyebrows lifted for a moment, and then he smiled a crooked smile. "What?"

She laughed, pleased that she'd succeeded in lightening the mood a little. "I think it's important to know my patients. Besides, if I want to color-code my files, knowing everyone's favorite color helps me do that. So, what's your answer to the big question?"

Dean laughed, and she noticed how kind his dark blue eyes looked. "Mmm, maybe red? Or sometimes blue. Like a dark blue."

"Like your eyes." She was about to say, but she stopped herself. Instead, she just nodded. "So red or blue. What about we just make things easy and say 'purple' for you?"

He laughed. "Sure. That's fine with me."

Chuckling, she made a note, feeling glad that she'd gotten him to laugh.

"What's your favorite color?" he asked, smiling that crooked smile again.

"Oh, me? Hmm, probably pink." She laughed.

"I can see that," he said, gesturing to the desk, which had a variety of pink items on it.

She found herself grinning. "But we're not here to talk about me. Let's go over the rest of your information. Tell me a little bit about your medical history." She wondered what it was that he was struggling with, since he didn't have any kind of visible injury.

He inhaled and then let out a long sigh. "Well, my health has been great for most of my life. I played sports as a kid and throughout high school. I own the local auto repair shop, so I do a lot of physical work on cars. But recently, I started feeling unusually fatigued and achy. Long story short, I went in to get tests done, and they came back with a diagnosis of osteoarthritis."

She watched his shoulders become tense as he spoke. She could tell that the unexpected diagnosis had turned his world upside down, and her heart went out to him.

"I'm so sorry to hear that," she said, meaning it sincerely. "Tell me more about what you do for a living. You said it's physically demanding work?"

"It can be. It involves heavy lifting and being in awkward positions underneath the cars sometimes." He laughed. "I love it, though. That's mostly why

I'm here. I'm hoping to improve my strength and flexibility so that I can go back to doing what I love. Cars are like giant puzzles, and putting them back together exactly the right way is important, rewarding work. Essentially what I'm doing is keeping the people in my community safe. That means a great deal to me."

She nodded, noting the passion in his voice when he spoke about his work. Her heart broke as she guessed how devastating it must be for a strong, athletic man like him to have to deal with the weakness and pain that came with osteoarthritis.

"It sounds as though you're a wonderful mechanic," she said, smiling at him. "You clearly have a passion for your work. Do you take all kinds of cars at your repair shop? Even older ones?"

He grinned. "Oh, yeah, we fix everything. My favorite was a 1968 Ford truck. We had to take apart the engine and put it back together again with some new parts, which was difficult because we had to search for them because they're antiques. But we ended up finding the parts we were looking for, and the whole thing was such a fun, rewarding experience."

"Really? That's fantastic. I tried to find a vintage alternator once, and it was very difficult."

His eyebrows lifted in surprise. "I didn't expect a physical therapist to have that kind of knowledge about cars. Do you work on cars?"

She laughed. "Not really. I mean, I know some things about fixing cars, and I enjoy the work. My grandpa loves cars and he taught me about them when I was a kid. I actually moved here to Rosewood Beach to be closer to my grandparents. My grandpa and I haven't worked too much on cars together since I came here, but when I was younger we restored a 1988 Porsche 911, and it was so much fun." She stared into space for a moment, reliving the memories in her mind. "I just remember feeling so proud of what we were doing, even though I never got to see the thing running."

"How come?" He no longer appeared uncomfortable or eager to leave. There was a sparkle of interest in his eyes, and she knew that they'd landed on a subject that fascinated him immensely.

She shook her head. "I was away at school when he finished it—he finally got the engine up and running. I was so sad about it at the time, because I'd never gotten to ride in it."

He nodded. "I can understand that. But at least you still had that wonderful experience with your grandfather."

"Oh, you're so right." She smiled at him warmly.

"That must have been hard, to go back and forth to your grandparents' like that," he said. "I'm lucky that my family has always been in the same place, at least for the most part. I have two sisters that moved away for a while, but they're both back now. Both my parents have always been here in Rosewood Beach with me—" He suddenly stopped himself. "Well, my father passed away recently. But up until then..."

She nodded quickly, feeling another surge of sympathy for him. "I'm so sorry for your loss."

"Thank you." He swallowed. He seemed to suddenly realize that he'd become unusually comfortable with her, sharing so much after knowing her for only a few minutes.

She could understand where he was coming from. She also felt instantly comfortable with him in a way that felt fun and easy. He was the kind of person that she would like to be friends with, she thought, and she was glad that there were people her own age like him in Rosewood Beach.

"Let's go ahead and get started," she said, smiling cheerfully. "We've introduced ourselves and gone over your medical information. Am I right in guessing that your goals are decreased pain, and increased strength and flexibility?"

He nodded, smiling. "Yeah, that's about the size of it. Whatever you can do to help me feel better, doctor."

"Sounds good." She smiled back at him. "Let's go ahead and get started."

She thought about how odd it was that she'd just decided she'd probably be dealing with mostly achy, geriatric hips and knees. She hadn't expected a young, charismatic man to be on her schedule. Although she loved working with elderly people, she found herself excited over the fact that she would get to be working with Dean as well. He seemed like a pleasant person who she would like to be friends with.

# CHAPTER EIGHT

Julia felt a warm breeze ruffle against her face, and droplets of cool water landed on her arms. The air was filled with the invigorating smell of chlorinated water, and she took a deep breath, smiling. The sounds of splashing and children laughing surrounded her, and she felt lighthearted and in a playful, energetic mood.

She and Cooper and Macey were at the Rosewood Beach splash pad, enjoying one of the last hot days of the year. Even though the sun was hot that day, there was still a certain scent in the air that hinted at autumn. It was gorgeous weather, Julia thought, and she felt thrilled to be able to spend time outside with people she loved.

"Is it fun, Macey?" she called to Cooper's

daughter, who was standing underneath a large plastic flower that was raining down waterdrops.

Macey, who was wearing a pink and yellow frilly bathing suit, laughed and clapped her hands. Julia's heart melted, and she felt an urge to scoop Macey up in her arms and give her a big squeeze. Since she herself wasn't wearing a bathing suit, however, she decided to stay where she was, away from the plastic flower's stream of water.

Cooper was standing closer to his daughter, hovering near her as if worried that she might fall. He was wearing jeans and a paint-flecked work shirt, but he'd gotten soaked by the splash pad already. Both he and Julia were barefoot, and he had his jeans rolled up almost to his knees. He was watching his daughter with a look of total adoration on his face, and Julia couldn't help grinning at the sight.

"You know what would make it ever more fun?" Julia asked Macey.

Macey looked up at her with big happy eyes, smiling expectantly.

"I think..." Julia took a couple of steps closer to Cooper and Macey. "That what would make it more fun... would be... a splash attack!"

Laughing, she bent down to splash Cooper and Macey with the shallow water of the splash pad. It was difficult to do, since there were only a few inches of water on the ground, but the way that Macey immediately started laughing was well worth the challenge.

"Oh, yeah?" Cooper laughed. "Retaliation!"

He grabbed Julia around the waist and tugged her under the spray of water coming from the plastic flower. She laughed hysterically as she tried to wiggle away from him, and then gave up. He dipped her back into a kiss, and she thought to herself that she never would have thought that getting kissed on a splash pad could feel so romantic.

She felt water splashing against her shins, and a moment later she and Cooper looked down to see Macey splashing them with water just like Julia had splashed her and Cooper a moment ago.

"Wow, you're a fast learner, Macey." Julia gave the little girl a high-five. "You're really good at splashing."

Macey offered her a chubby smile, and Cooper picked his daughter up and gave her a big squeeze, just like Julia had wanted to earlier. He kissed Macey on the cheek and danced with her under the spray of water for a little while. Julia's heart warmed as she watched the two of them, and she thought to herself that she couldn't wait until her bond with the little girl was even stronger.

Finally, Macey started to wiggle out of Cooper's arms, so he set her down on the ground.

"I think she wants to play with those toddlers," Cooper said, nodding toward a group of little kids who were sitting down in a section of the splash pad that had squirts of water fountaining up from the ground.

He led Macey over to where the other kids were, and then he took Julia's hand.

"Let's sit on this bench right here," he suggested. "I don't feel the need to be so close to her now that she's sitting down. She isn't going to slip and fall."

Julia smiled, glad for a chance to talk with her boyfriend for a while. They settled down comfortably on the bench, watching the way Macey was splashing happily with the other children.

"Oh, she's a sweetheart." Julia gazed at the toddler, feeling her heart ache with love.

"She's a scamp." Cooper laughed. "I'm completely soaked."

"Mmm, I'm pretty sure you did most of that to yourself. Like when you were holding me underneath the stream of water."

Cooper grinned and leaned back against the bench. "Oh, that was well worth it."

She laughed and wrapped her arms around him, and he kissed her affectionately.

"So tell me how you've been," he said. "How have things been going at the pub?"

"Oh, it's a whirlwind as always. Not a day does by when we don't have some kind of bizarre problem." She laughed. "But it's always fun. We've got a great team—we're so great at putting out fires, I think I'm going to buy everyone little medals that say, 'Champion Firefighter.'"

He laughed at her joke. "What kind of fires? Do you run low on supplies?"

"Oh, nothing like that. Mom's so good at making sure we have everything we need in stock, and the cooks are great at communicating when we're unusually low on something."

"So what kind of things go wrong?" His brows furrowed curiously.

"Oh, where to begin?" She laughed. "Sometimes things go wrong with the building itself, like the day that we found out we had a wasp nest in the corner of the patio. Thankfully no one got stung, but there were some close calls and some unhappy customers."

"I remember hearing about that," he said, shaking his head sympathetically.

"From whom? Us or one of the unhappy customers?"

He laughed. "I believe it was my beautiful girlfriend who told me about it."

"You have a beautiful girlfriend? Wow. What are you doing hanging out with me?"

"Yup, the prettiest girlfriend in the world." He gave her a kiss, and her heart swelled with affection for him. "So anyway, tell me more about these fires."

"Hmm. Well, one day one of the teenage waiters knocked over a bag of flour in storage. The whole room was covered in a film of white dust, and it took us hours to clean it up that night after the pub closed."

"Couldn't you just leave things a little dusty?"

She shook her head. "We offer gluten-free options at the pub, which means we need to ensure that some things the guests are eating don't have gluten in them. We can't cook with things that are covered in a film of flour without a little flour getting into all of the food."

He nodded. "Makes sense. Wow. I bet that kid felt bad."

"Oh, he did." She chuckled. "But we were nice about it. And he stayed to help us clean it all up. That's the last time he wasn't careful in the storage room, let me tell you. Oh, and then..." She put a hand to her mouth to stifle a laugh as another incident rose up in her mind. "Mrs. Billings was in one afternoon, and Alexis saw her putting salt into her coffee. You know, like a salt packet instead of a sugar packet. Alexis didn't have time to stop her and then she felt like she should just keep her mouth shut so Mrs. Billings didn't get embarrassed. But then when Mrs. Billings tasted her coffee, she said it was the worst coffee she'd ever had and made a whole scene. Alexis had to point out that she'd used the salt packet, which was still lying on the table, and everyone was staring." Julia wiped a tear away. "Mrs. Billings left her a twenty-dollar tip that day."

Cooper chuckled. "Well, at least she was nice about it in the end."

She nodded. "But I think customers bring the most chaos to the pub. Which is probably to be expected. George Melder keeps trying to bring his dog into the pub. We have to keep explaining to him that because his chihuahua isn't registered as a service animal, she isn't allowed inside because of people's allergies and because some kids are scared of dogs. Well, anyway, it's gotten to the point where he's been sneaking her inside in his jacket. She sits in the corner of the booth next to him and he sneaks her bites of his food. It's so cute that usually we just turn a blind eye to it and take care to wipe the booth out when they've left."

"Oh, I'd love to see that." He grinned. "Next time it happens, tell me and I'll run over there so I can witness it."

She grinned back at him. "It's every Thursday afternoon for lunch, at noon exactly. You could set your clock by George."

They both chuckled, and then they fell quiet for a few moments. Julia turned to watch Macey, feeling delighted by how happy the little girl was.

"Are you sure you still like it here, Julia?"

She turned to her boyfriend in surprise. His expression had grown serious, and she grabbed his hand. "What do you mean?"

"Well, I know you have fun at the pub, but Rosewood Beach is such a big change from New York. I just wondered if sometimes you miss the big city. I'm sure people are more sophisticated there."

He cocked an eyebrow as he said the last bit, imitating someone fancy, and she laughed.

"Oh, I can assure you, there are just as many

characters in New York as there are here in Rosewood Beach," she told him. "Probably more, actually. And I would never want it any other way. Sometimes people make trouble, but they keep things interesting too. And I love my job. I love fighting for the progress of something I care about, not just numbers on paper. I can literally get my hands dirty at the pub, working hard to make sure it's doing well. I love that. And I love working with my family." Her tone took on a tender quality as she added, "And besides, *you're* not in New York. I love being here with you."

His expression softened. "I'm so glad you're here."

She kissed him. "There is no place I would rather be."

Their attention was abruptly drawn to Macey when the little girl let out a squeal of displeasure. One of the other children had probably splashed her with water, and her face was scrunched up as if she was close to tears.

"Uh oh," Cooper said, standing up. "I guess it's time for dinner."

He went back onto the splash pad and scooped Macey up into his arms. The little girl leaned her head against his shoulder in a way that made Julia's heart melt.

"Are you ready to go home and eat some dinner, Macey?" Cooper asked her, kissing the top of her head.

"Yeah," Macey said, and yawned.

"I'd be tired too if I just had that much fun." Julia reached out to smooth an errant lock of the girl's hair. "Sometimes fun can be exhausting."

Cooper chuckled, and they turned toward the entrance to the splash pad, ready to get back into his car and head to his house. A few moments later, however, someone called Cooper's name eagerly.

They turned and saw a family approaching them. The man had a thick black mustache and Julia thought he looked familiar. Next to him was his smiling wife and two kids, both of whom were a few years older than Macey.

"Dave!" Cooper grinned and shook the other man's hand in a friendly manner. "I haven't seen you in, gosh, two hours?"

Dave laughed. "Thought you were rid of me for the day, didn't you?"

Julia chuckled. It was clear that this was one of Cooper's co-workers, and she enjoyed seeing the friendly camaraderie that the two of them shared.

Cooper grinned. "This is my daughter Macey, and my girlfriend Julia."

"Macey I've met, Julia I think I might have seen around before." Dave shook Julia's hand. "This is my wife Stacey and our kids, Harrison and Levi."

Stacey and Julia smiled at each other and shook hands. The kids looked up at Julia and Cooper a bit warily.

"Are you coming bowling with the rest of the guys tonight?" Dave asked Cooper. "Should be a great time. Tony wants to celebrate his tenth year with Greener Pastures, so he offered to buy everyone pizza."

"Bowling?" Cooper looked confused.

"Yeah, have you seen the group chat? He just suggested it about an hour ago, but it sounds like almost everyone is in. You should come by. I hear you're a mean bowler."

"Oh, I haven't seen the thread. I haven't checked my phone in about an hour and a half."

"Too busy watching that one, huh?" Dave nodded his head toward Macey, who had fallen asleep on Cooper's shoulder. "She looks like a little wild one."

Cooper laughed. "She might look like an angel right now, but she is a wild one sometimes."

"You should go, Cooper." Julia smiled at him. "That sounds like a lot of fun."

Cooper glanced hesitantly down at Macey. "I can't bring Macey with me to a bowling alley, not when she's so tired like this."

"Don't worry about it!" Julia touched his arm. "I'll take care of her for the evening. I'll make her dinner and read her stories and tuck her into bed. We'll have a great time, and you can spend time with the guys."

Cooper swallowed, clearly hesitating. Then he shook his head. "Thank you for offering, sweetheart, but she's so tired tonight and she's been a bit sad lately. I think it's best if I do the usual bedtime routine with her." He smiled sweetly at her. "But I appreciate you being willing to do that."

Julia's heart sank. Although Cooper was being as sweet as always, she wished that he treated her more equally when it came to taking care of Macey. She found herself wondering what it might be like if she and Cooper ever got married. Would he still insist on taking care of Macey even when Julia could tap in and do it for him? Would she always be the "non-parent"?

"Another time, Dave." Cooper smiled at his

friend. "Give Tony my congratulations. Ten years is a big deal."

Dave sighed, although he was still smiling. "Oh well, more pizza for us, I guess. Have a good night, Cooper."

"You too."

Waving goodbye, Cooper and Julia started to walk toward the parking lot again. She couldn't help feeling sad and disappointed. She wished that Cooper trusted her more to take care of his daughter, and she wished that she was able to spend more quality time with Macey.

"You okay, sweetheart?" Cooper asked her when they were almost to the car. She realized that he had been watching her as they walked, and his expression looked worried.

"Oh! Yes, of course. Everything's fine." She put on a smile. "Why?"

"Well, you're acting quiet, that's all." He smiled back, but his eyes looked a little troubled, as if he didn't quite buy her answer.

She considered bringing up her frustrations for a moment, but then she decided that she didn't want to mess up a lovely day. "I'm just tired, I guess. Like I said to Macey, sometimes having fun can really tire you out."

He laughed and slipped his hand around hers. She smiled at him, repressing a sigh. She told herself to be grateful that she got to spend the evening with him and Macey, but she couldn't help wishing that he was willing to let her care for his daughter more.

# CHAPTER NINE

Dean stood on the front step of Alexis and Grayson's new house and rang the doorbell. He heard the sound of chimes echoing faintly in the beautiful old house, and he smiled quietly to himself. He felt glad that Alexis and Grayson had found such a beautiful home to settle down in. It was hardly as glamorous as their massive mansion in L.A. had been, which he'd been to one time and legitimately gotten lost in, but it was just the right size for a couple who might have children one day. It was large enough to be spacious, and small enough to be cozy.

While he waited for his sister to come to the door, he glanced at the garden, admiring how well-tended it was. Although most of the flowers had wilted, there was still green life in the flower beds, and they were orderly and tidy. He knew that the garden had been in great condition when Alexis had purchased the house, but it was clear that she'd lovingly kept up the flower beds.

The front door opened, and Alexis appeared, grinning affectionately. She was wearing jeans and a comfortable-looking oversized dress shirt which he guessed might belong to Grayson. Her reddish-brown hair was pulled back into a messy bun, and her eyes were bright with energy.

"Dean! Just the man I wanted to see."

"Here I am, your friendly neighborhood technician," he said, laughing. "Explain to me again what you want me to fix?"

"Well, first come inside and eat a pumpkin scone and drink the glass of apple juice I poured for you."

"Wow, free snacks? I should come fix things at your house more often."

She laughed. "I had to pay you back for coming all the way out here somehow."

"I wouldn't call a five-minute drive 'all the way out here.'"

"Just shush and eat the scone," she said, handing him a plate.

"Yes, ma'am." He chuckled and took a bite out of

the scone, which was rich and buttery. "Mm, thank you, that's fantastic."

"Isn't it?" She laughed. "Thanks. Hazel gave me the recipe."

"Hazel is a baking wizard, and I'm happy to see that she's spreading her magic." He took another bite, savoring the taste. "Now that I've been paid in snacks, what's the issue with your TV?"

"It's not the TV, it's the Roku device. The Wi-Fi is refusing to connect, and the remote is being temperamental."

"Oh, those remotes. They're just like teenagers."

Alexis laughed so hard at his joke that she snorted, and Dean grinned before taking a refreshing sip of the apple juice.

"But seriously, Dean, we can't get it to work. Grayson is a brilliant man, but he can't figure out electronics to save his life." Her voice rose in volume a little bit as she talked about Grayson, and her teasing tone implied that she meant for him to hear her say it.

Dean laughed. "Well, luckily for your marriage, I should be able to figure it out. Happy to help. Where is it?"

"Before—well, I wanted to ask you." All at once

her expression became serious. "Are you sure you're up for it? I don't want to tire you out."

Dean gave her a look.

She nodded. "Okay." She didn't say any more about it, and he was glad that he'd been able to communicate his feelings to her with just a look. He was grateful that his family wanted to take care of him, but he also didn't want to be treated like an invalid, or someone who wasn't able to make their own decisions properly. If he'd been feeling too tired to come to Alexis's house to work on her technology, he would have told her so.

"Lead me to the device," he said, smiling at her.

She led him into the charming, cozy living room, where the Roku device was set up underneath the TV.

"See what you can make of it," she said with a sigh. "I hope it's not just broken. Then we'll have to go buy a new one."

"I bet it's okay," he said, crouching down and beginning to inspect the small device.

"Hey, Dean!" Grayson appeared in the living room, also munching on one of the scones. "Good to see you. Thanks for coming over here to help us out."

"You got it." Dean grinned at him.

"We need you to save us, because Alexis never lets me try to fix anything."

Alexis laughed and patted Grayson's face fondly. "It's just that I knew that Dean would know exactly what was wrong. It's not that I don't believe in you, it's just that... well, you remember how long it took when our internet was down." She shook her head wryly.

"Hey, I tried what the guy on the phone said—"

Alexis lifted a brow at him. "Speaking of phone calls, isn't your mother expecting a call from you?"

Grayson chuckled. "Very smooth." He kissed his wife's cheek. "You're right. I'll be in the other room if you need me."

"I always need you." She grinned at him.

"Except for when technology isn't working, then you need your brother."

"Nope, I still need you."

Alexis and Grayson kissed, and Dean let out a cheerful, "Eew!"

"Okay, okay, I'm leaving." Grayson laughed. "Good luck, Dean!"

"Thanks." Dean smiled cheerfully from his spot on the floor. He was amused by how cute Alexis and Grayson were acting. Once Grayson had left the living room, he turned to his sister with a smile. "Things are going well, huh?"

She nodded. "With Grayson? Oh, absolutely. It's wonderful having my husband back. He's treating me like he used to when we were dating—no, actually, he's treating me with even more affection than he did when we were dating."

Something about the way she'd responded made him curious. "What about things other than Grayson? Is that all good too?"

"Yeah." She hesitated slightly before answering. "Things are going well generally too."

Dean stopped looking at the Roku device. He placed his hands on his knees and looked up at his sister. "Tell me what's on your mind. I can tell that something is off. You can talk to me about it."

She shook her head. "It's really nothing." She smiled at him. "Things are going so well at the pub. We've got happy customers, and Julia says the finances are getting better and better all the time. I feel so proud of what we've all accomplished since Dad passed. And you remember Judd McCormick?"

Dean pretended to shudder. "Who could forget the man who tried to bully our mother into selling the family business?"

"Well, the word on the street is that the McCormicks are extremely jealous of how things have picked up at The Lighthouse Grill. I mean, Judd was so sure that we weren't going to be able to keep the pub because of Dad's debts, but we overcame that challenge, and now the pub's finances are doing better than ever before. I think it's because Julia has been handling the finances so well. She's practically a wizard at it."

"I agree with you." Dean grinned. "And I'm glad that Judd and his sons are jealous. That's a one-sided rivalry, and we absolutely deserve to thrive in spite of them."

"Why are they like that, anyway?" she asked, sitting down next to him on the floor. "Judd isn't exactly mean-spirited, but he's so entitled. Why did he act like he deserved to take our place just because he wanted it?"

Dean shrugged. "Some people are like that, I guess. They're brought up to be selfish and they never learn how to be any other way. Although, the one McCormick son is different. Seth and Brady work for their father at the brewery, but Ryan works for a construction firm. I've hung out with Ryan a few times; he's a good guy. He's not like the rest of the family."

"Huh. I guess that's proof that anyone can be a

good person even if they're not brought up that way."
She smiled at her brother. "Well, good for Ryan."

"Yeah, but there's still something that's bothering you, I can tell. I can agree that the pub is going great, and you've seemed to love working there. But do you? Are you getting tired of it?"

She shook her head. "No, I still love working there. But..."

"Ah, there is it! Come on, out with it. What's on your mind?"

She laughed. "For a while, I didn't even know what was bothering me. I felt as though something was missing, but I couldn't figure out what it was. Now I've realized that I'm missing my creative outlet."

"That makes sense. You've always been a really creative person. I'll never forget that time you made an entire Noah's Ark out of papier-mâché."

She grinned. "Oh, I remember that. The pigs were my favorite. They were so cute and roly-poly."

"They did look amazing. And you were like, twelve, and that's impressive. You're really good at creating stuff, Alexis. You should figure out ways to scratch that creative itch. Why don't you pick up some old hobbies as a way of getting your creative juices flowing?"

"You mean I should make another Noah's Ark out of papier-mâché?"

He laughed. "Only if you want to. Do something that you really enjoy, that lets you feel creative. I always go out and find a fixer-upper car to work on when I feel like I need a creative release. It's such a challenge that it feels like playing a video game or something." He paused, suddenly feeling a wave of sadness as he thought about how his hands had a hard time getting through a regular workday now. He didn't know if he would be able to do extra car work during his time off from work anymore. His heart sank as he thought about how that had been his favorite hobby, and he didn't want to give it up.

*Don't say never, Dean*, he reminded himself. *Your strength might improve. Wait and see.*

"Hey." Alexis placed a hand on his shoulder, as if she could guess that the challenges of his diagnosis were troubling him. "I think things are going to get better for you. And you shouldn't ignore the possibility that going to physical therapy might drastically improve your symptoms. You should really make an appointment, Dean."

He lifted one shoulder in a shrug. "I already did."

She let out a little yelp of excitement. "You

what? You're a fine one for secrets! That's amazing. I'm so proud of you."

He shook his head, laughing. "You act like I'd vowed to never set foot in a physical therapy clinic ever in my life."

She grinned. "I know how stubborn men can be. And besides, I know it was something you felt torn about. So I am, I'm really proud of you for going. How was it?"

He shrugged. "It went well, I suppose." He thought about his visit to the clinic and smiled a little when he thought about Noelle. She had been so kind and considerate. He'd had a great time talking with her. He wasn't sure how he had expected physical therapy to be, but his session with Noelle had been so unexpectedly pleasant. Noelle had been insightful, and she'd seemed to genuinely care about his passions and interests. Then again, he reflected, she must be like that with everyone.

"Oh, come on." She laughed. "Please tell me more. What was it like? Do you think it'll help you?"

"It was fine. The physical therapist is very nice, and she seems to really know what she's doing. It's too early to tell if it'll really help me or not, but I'll keep trying it. But only because I'm outnumbered by women who insist on badgering me about it."

He grinned as he said the last part, softening his expression so that she'd know it was a joke.

She smiled back and hugged him around the shoulders. "I'm so happy to hear that. I just know it's going to change your life."

He chuckled, but inwardly he thought that that was probably an exaggeration. He doubted that it would really change his life. He did feel hopeful, however. As much as he liked to tease about it, he felt grateful that his sisters had pushed him toward going to physical therapy.

If anything could help him feel better, it would be that, and he was glad that someone as kind and capable as Noelle was guiding him through the process.

# CHAPTER TEN

Noelle whistled quietly to herself as she bustled around in the kitchen of her cozy apartment. She had old folk music playing through a little speaker on her kitchen counter, and she was whistling along to the music cheerfully. Sunlight spilled through the windows, making the colored glass vases that she kept lined up on the windowsill gleam charmingly.

"Oh, strawberries," she murmured, and opened the refrigerator.

She was in the middle of packing herself a picnic lunch for the day. It was a beautiful, crisp Saturday morning, and she'd decided to visit one of Rosewood Beach's landmarks, a shallow cave in a hill tucked between the water and a grove of birch trees. It was called the Sea Captain's Closet, since when it had been discovered, a chest of antique sailor's clothes had been found in it. Noelle found caves thrilling and a little spooky, and she was looking forward to exploring this one, even though it didn't go very far into the side of the hill.

She'd decided to pack herself a lunch and make a day of it. She'd made herself a chicken sandwich with tomato and avocado slices, and she'd already packed a couple of oatmeal raisin cookies that she'd made the day before. Her coffee, improved with cream and a shot of caramel syrup, was ready to go in a travel mug. As soon as she'd remembered the sweet strawberries that she had in the refrigerator, she'd decided she wanted to bring some of those along as well.

She rinsed them off and tucked them into a little Tupperware, which she placed into her lunch box next to her sandwich and the cookies.

*Looks like I'm just about ready to go*, she thought cheerfully. *I can't wait.*

She glanced out the window at the sunny day, thinking to herself that it was a perfect day for this kind of excursion. She hurried into her bedroom and opened her closet, taking out a baseball cap and a sweater, since she guessed that it would become chillier later in the day.

She tied the sweater around her waist and wiggled the baseball cap onto her head. She looked at her reflection in the mirror, thinking cheerfully to herself that she looked ready for an adventure. She was wearing hiking boots, jeans, and a long-sleeved t-shirt. Her light brown hair was pulled back into a low ponytail which highlighted its soft waves.

She let out a sigh of satisfaction and went back into the kitchen to get her lunchbox and coffee thermos. She left her apartment with a spring in her step and got into her car. She was just pulling out of the parking lot when she noticed that her brakes felt strangely unstable. She had to push her foot very firmly against the pedal in order to get the car to stop.

*That doesn't feel right at all*, she thought, alarmed. *I can't drive anywhere if there's an issue with my brakes.*

She groaned. Car difficulties always flustered her, and this was making her feel especially worried —not to mention disappointed.

"Oh, I hope it's some kind of easy fix," she muttered as she pulled over on the side of the road. "I don't want to miss out on the lovely day I had planned."

She pulled her phone out of her pocket and quickly looked up the nearest auto repair shop. It was only a three-minute drive away, and she breathed a sigh of relief.

She carefully eased her car back out into the road and made her way to the shop. She bit her lip the whole way, wondering what was wrong with her car and hoping it didn't suddenly stop working altogether or explode.

She breathed a sigh of relief as she pulled into the parking lot of the auto repair shop. By that point, it was very difficult to get her car to stop. She got out and hurried inside, finding herself in a cool, plainly decorated lobby that featured a tire display in one corner and several blue armchairs.

She rang a desk bell on the front counter, and a moment later a smiling young man with "Keith" written on his nametag stepped into the room.

"Hi there," he said. "What can we help you with today?"

"The brakes on my car are acting strange," she told him. "I was having trouble stopping the car by the time I got here."

He asked her a few questions and she answered them, and he nodded, frowning in concern.

"Sounds like maybe your brake lines have a leak or got snapped somehow," he said. "We'll bring your car into the shop and take a look at it."

"Sounds great, thank you. Do you want me to drive it in, or... ?"

"I'll bring it in." He held out his hand, and for a second she thought he was asking for a high-five, and she felt confused and inclined to laugh. Then she realized that he was asking her to hand him her keys so that he could move her car.

"Yes! Oh, sorry." She laughed, rummaging in her purse and feeling flustered and amused. She was clearly out of it, rattled by her concerns for her vehicle. "Here you are. Any guesses as to how long that will take?"

He shook his head. "I can't say for sure. First thing is we should run a diagnostic on your car and figure out what's wrong with it. Then we can let you know about repairs and cost and how long it will probably take." He smiled, and she forced herself to smile back, even though she could feel herself wanting to wiggle with impatience.

*Oh, I hope it doesn't take too long,* she thought as she followed Keith outside. *I really want to get to that cave today, and before my lunch spoils!*

She watched with her hands clasped behind her back as Keith drove her car into the garage. She saw him frowning in concentration, but he was also able to stop it.

She wasn't sure if she was allowed in the garage as a customer or not, but she didn't see anyone besides Keith in there, so she tiptoed inside. The garage smelled strongly of gasoline, oil, and grease, and she smiled quietly to herself. She loved those smells, because they made her think of repairing cars with her grandfather.

Keith got out of her car, and she stood near him.

"Did it stop okay?" she asked anxiously. She tended to hover when she was nervous about something. It was as if she was watching some suspenseful movie or reading a gripping book, and she couldn't bring herself to look away from the unfolding action.

"Not too good, but I managed it. You can go ahead and sit in the lobby, ma'am. I'll take a look at your car and come back inside to let you know what needs to be done about it."

"I think I'd rather just watch you do it," she said. "It won't take all that long, will it?"

Keith glanced at her, looking hesitant. "Well, we don't usually have customers here in the shop."

"Oh, I won't get in your way. I'll just watch. I mean, I trust you, it isn't that. Is that okay?"

He hesitated again, and then nodded. "Okay, I guess so."

Keith began to inspect her car, starting by opening the hood. Noelle watched nervously as he began to check the levels of various fluid containers.

"Are they okay?" she asked, stepping forward. "That brake fluid is low, isn't it?"

He turned to her in surprise. "Yeah, that's the brake fluid and it is low. You probably have a damaged brake line. Let me check some other things here."

He continued to do a thorough inspection of her engine and the surrounding parts, and even though she was grateful that he was being so careful, she wished it didn't take so long. She found herself inching forward to look over his shoulder until she was standing directly behind him.

Then all at once, someone tapped her on the shoulder. "Ma'am, I'll have to ask you to back up."

She whirled around, startled, and her jaw dropped when she saw Dean Owens standing there behind her. In the next instant, his eyebrows lifted with recognition.

"Oh! Noelle! I—you—"

"My goodness!" she spluttered, feeling surprised but delighted. "What are you—no, this is your shop?"

He grinned and shrugged. "Guilty. I mean, it's the only auto repair shop in town."

"It is?" She laughed. "I didn't realize that. I just went to the nearest one. I mean, not that I wouldn't have wanted to come to your shop. I would have come here on purpose if it wasn't an emergency, but it's a—well, we're not sure exactly what's wrong yet—"

She realized she was rambling a little, feeling flustered by seeing Dean suddenly appear behind her like that. He was wearing a blue mechanic's jumpsuit, and he looked professional and energetic, so different from the tired-looking man who had first stepped inside her office at the clinic.

"You're all good." He waved a calloused hand. "What's the emergency? Something not working with your car?"

"Yeah, the brakes." Keith grimaced good-naturedly. "Good thing she came in here right away."

"The brakes aren't working?" Dean turned to Noelle in alarm. "But you're okay?"

She nodded, feeling touched by his concern. "I mean, they're still functional. But they're starting to be very difficult to use. Keith said the brake lines were probably damaged."

"Ah." Dean nodded sympathetically. "Well, the good news is, we can fix that. Why don't you go ahead and wait in my office while we take a look at this thing? Then we can let you know if that's the issue for sure, and if there are any other issues as well."

"Oh, I hope not!" She laughed breathlessly. "But sure, thank you. I'm sorry, I suppose I was getting in the way out here."

"Don't worry about it, I know you meant well." Dean smiled at her. "It's just that there's a lot that goes on out here and sometimes repairing cars can be dangerous. It's our company policy that guests aren't allowed in the garage."

"I understand." She smiled back at him.

"Let me show you where my office is. There's a coffee pot with fresh coffee in there. Feel free to help yourself if you like."

"Oh, thank you." She glanced at her car, where her coffee thermos was tucked into the cupholder. It might be a while before she got to drink out of it. "That sounds nice, maybe I will."

"And there's cream and sugar in a little basket next to it. I'm not particularly cutesy like that myself, but I have a mother and three sisters." He chuckled, and she grinned at him.

As she followed him across the garage to his office, she found herself wondering if his mother and sisters were the only women in his life, or if he had a girlfriend too. He seemed like a very nice guy, dependable and hard-working. It was clear that he ran his auto repair shop responsibly and with genuine care for his employees and his customers.

"Here it is," he said, pushing open the door of his office.

It was a small room, clean and comfortable, with a swivel chair behind the desk, a small bookshelf filled with car manuals, a couple of chairs set against the wall, and a small table with a coffee machine and a mug tree resting on the top of it.

"What a nice office," she said, meaning it genuinely.

"Thank you." He smiled at her. "You can sit down in any of the chairs, but I recommend the swivel chair. It's more comfortable. And more fun."

She laughed and watched as he shut the office door behind him. Finding herself alone, she turned slowly around the room, examining it more closely.

She thought to herself that it was nice to be able to see Dean in his element, where he could show her his area of expertise. It leveled the playing field between them a bit—she was no longer the only one who was offering the other help. Now she'd come to him for help too.

She poured herself a cup of coffee and added

hazelnut creamer. She began to stroll slowly around the room, looking at the photographs that were hanging on the walls. She was curious to learn more about Dean and his life, and although she didn't quite admit it to herself, she was also looking to see if there were any pictures of a girlfriend on the walls.

There were some girls in the photographs, but they resembled Dean so much that she guessed they were his sisters. She smiled as she looked at them, thinking that they looked like very nice women, the kind of women who she'd like to be friends with.

She saw a photo of a baseball team cheering, clearly celebrating a victory, and she picked out Dean's smiling face in the crowd of teammates. There were photos of car shows, of fishing trips, and a picture of Dean standing on the top of a bluff with his arms held up as if in celebration that he'd made it.

She bit her lip, struck by how energetic and healthy he looked in all of the pictures. Seeing him like that increased her determination to make things better for him through PT.

"I was pretty skinny, wasn't I?"

She jumped, startled, and whirled around to see Dean standing in the doorway, grinning at her. A drop of coffee splashed onto her hand, and she wiped it off, laughing.

"Oops, sorry." He grinned apologetically. "That's the second time I've scared you today."

"No, it's okay." She chuckled. "I guess I'm just a little embarrassed you caught me snooping."

"You're not snooping. Those pictures were hung up to be looked at. Did you see the one of the fishing trip? I didn't catch that monster, but I wish I had. That was the biggest fish I've ever seen with my own eyes."

"I did see it." She grinned. "Very impressive. What's the verdict on my car, doctor?"

"Oh, not so good." He sighed. "One of the brake lines snapped and will need to be replaced. You've also got a leak in your coolant, which needs to be fixed or your engine could overheat. We can fix both of those things for you, but it'll take us the rest of the day."

Disappointment flopped in Noelle's stomach. "It will? You're sure?"

He nodded. "Unfortunately. We're making your car as much of a priority as we can, since you came in with a safety concern, but we also have other car repair appointments we have to honor. I can promise you that we'll get it done before tomorrow, though. Did you have somewhere you needed to be today?"

She shook her head. "Needed is the wrong word.

I had a hike and a picnic planned for today, but it will have to wait."

"Oh. Did—was someone else going with you, who could—"

She shook her head, smiling. "No, a solo expedition I'm afraid. I wanted to see the Sea Captain's Closet today. I was trying to get to know Rosewood Beach better, since I just moved here recently."

"I'm sorry." He smiled sympathetically. "The good news is that there are plenty of other great places around town that are within walking distance. There are some parks, and there's an award-winning garden behind the library. Plenty of good places for a picnic."

"Thanks for the advice." She felt grateful that he was being so sweet about the whole thing. "I guess I should get my lunch box out of my car. Or... am I not allowed back in the garage?"

He laughed at her joke, shaking his head. "Nah, I can make an exception in your case. Feel free to grab your stuff, and then if you could meet me back in here, we'll get some of the paperwork out of the way. Mostly I just need your phone number so we can call you when your car is ready."

"Sounds good."

She smiled at him and went back out into the garage to get her stuff. She exchanged a few friendly words with Keith, and then returned to Dean's office, where he'd prepared a couple of documents for her to sign.

"I hope the price is okay," he said, handing the papers to her. "Maybe I could give you a physical therapist's discount." He chuckled.

"Oh, thanks for offering, but that looks more than fair." She smiled at him as she sat down. "And I'm just so grateful you're able to fix my car on short notice. My apartment is only a three-minute drive from here, so I'm so relieved I didn't have to drive far with my brakes acting up like that."

He nodded. "Always err on the side of caution for that sort of thing. It's usually best to get a tow to be on the safe side. Although, I trust you to make smart decisions about things like that. You seem like a cautious person."

She smiled as she signed the document. "I am careful. My job hinges so much around safety. I usually have safety on my brain."

"Me too." He chuckled.

For a moment, they sat there smiling at each other, and then finally she snapped herself out of it.

"Well, here you go." She stood up, handing him

the papers. She felt as though she'd like to stay and talk to him longer, but she guessed that he was busy and had a great deal to do. Besides, if she was going to go out and explore Rosewood Beach on foot, she should get a move on so that she could locate some picturesque spot by lunchtime.

"We'll give you a call. Have a good time exploring our town."

She smiled. "I will! I'll just have to explore the Sea Captain's Closet another time."

"You should. I've been there, it's pretty cool."

She thanked him again as she left his office and made her way outside. As she stepped back out into the sunshine, she found herself wondering about Dean. When had he gone to the cave? Had he been there a lot? Did he enjoy hiking as much as he seemed to enjoy working on cars and playing baseball?

She strolled along the sidewalk, swinging her lunch box from her hand and deciding she would just let her feet take her where they would. It was pleasant, she realized, to just let herself wander around without a specific agenda. She found herself noticing more of the details surrounding her than she normally would, such as a little gnome holding a pie in a front garden, and the smell of cinnamon and coffee wafting out of a gift shop.

She ended up in a small park at lunch time, where she ate her meal sitting at a picnic bench and looking out across the sparkling waves.

She found herself thinking about Dean again. She'd really admired the way he ran his business, and she could tell that he'd put a lot of years of hard work into it. She felt determined to help his quality of life improve, so that he had the energy to do all the things he liked to do.

When she was done with her lunch, she continued to wander around Rosewood Beach. She saw many beautiful things, and had an energizing, relaxing afternoon. No matter where she went or what she did, however, she kept thinking about Dean.

# CHAPTER ELEVEN

Alexis pushed open the glass front doors of the
Rosewood Beach General Store and took a deep
breath. She loved the smell of the general store. It
was always a pleasant mixture of nutty smells, from
things like boxes of cookies and fresh-baked loaves of
bread, and fresh smells, like the basil and sage plants
that were displayed on a table near the front
entrance.

She was there to buy supplies for the pub, and it
was an errand that she always enjoyed. She grabbed
a cart and began to weave her way through the aisles
of the store, pausing now and again to admire
something that caught her interest.

She was halfway done with her shopping when

she came across an aisle that contained jewelry making supplies. For a moment, she stared at the wires and the beautiful strands of colorful beads, enraptured by how lovely they looked.

*I used to love making jewelry*, she remembered. *I made those earrings in high school for Mom—they looked amazing.*

She stood looking at the beads for a moment, her mind beginning to whirr with ideas. Then she smiled and began to pick out some of the jewelry making supplies. She got the essentials along with a few strands of colorful glass beads.

She'd been wanting a creative outlet. Perhaps this could be it.

Feeling excited, she finished up the rest of her shopping. She dropped the majority of her purchases off at the pub and then went straight home. Once she was back inside her kitchen, she sat down at the kitchen table and spread her jewelry making supplies out across it. She smiled as she looked at the beads gleaming in the light.

Within a few seconds, she got an idea for a pair of earrings. Her hands began to work busily as her creative juices flowed. She turned on some soft jazz music to listen to as she worked, and before long, she'd created a charming pair of red and pink beaded earrings.

After what seemed like only a short amount of time, she'd also created a bracelet with an intricate beaded pattern. She smiled as she looked at it, feeling thrilled, and then she glanced at the clock hanging on the wall and noticed the time.

"Five thirty!" she gasped, and then started to laugh. She could hardly believe that two hours had passed since she'd started working.

*I guess I should stop and start cooking dinner,* she thought, looking down at her work with satisfaction. *I did an impressive amount of work in only two hours —and it was so much fun I barely felt time passing.*

She stood up and practically waltzed to the kitchen counter to start preparing a Shepherd's Pie. She hummed as she got vegetables and potatoes out of the refrigerator.

Crafting jewelry had felt wonderful. She had a sense of elation knowing that she had discovered something that fulfilled her urge to be creative.

* * *

Dean stepped back from Noelle's car and inspected it. He'd finished repairing her brake lines and her coolant and also changed her oil, which had been slightly overdue. Now he was working on waxing the outside of her car, wanting it to look clean and shiny. He was only charging her for the brake lines and the coolant, and everything else he was doing for free. He'd texted her to let her know her car was ready, and he was trying to spruce up as much of it as he could while she was on her way back to her apartment. He'd texted her earlier and offered to drop it off to her there, since that was a courtesy his shop often extended to customers. When she'd said that she was still out exploring, he'd asked if she wanted him to meet her where she was, but she'd said that she would be back to her apartment soon, and that it was probably the best landmark for him to shoot for.

He chuckled as he thought about her text. He liked the breezy, cheerful manner with which she communicated. She definitely had a fun, optimistic quality to her.

He went back to waxing and polishing, and he found himself thinking about the outfit she had been wearing that morning. She'd looked laid-back and adventurous but feminine at the same time. He'd liked her pink baseball cap. He smiled, thinking that the casual look had been very becoming on her, although she looked great in scrubs too.

"You want me to drop that off to her, boss?" Keith walked up to Dean.

"No, that's okay, I can do it." Dean smiled. "Thanks."

Keith looked down at Dean's hands and frowned. "Look, I don't mean to put my oar in here, but your hands are shaking. And it's past the time when you usually go home."

Dean looked down at his hands, surprised. He hadn't even realized they'd been shaking. He wondered if he hadn't noticed because he'd become so used to the sensation, or because he'd been so preoccupied with thinking about Noelle. "Ah, I guess you're right. Thank you, I appreciate it. I'll let you do the honors."

"No problem." Keith smiled and clapped Dean on the back. "See you on Monday, boss."

"See you Monday." Dean smiled at Keith, who climbed into Noelle's car, where the keys were resting on the dashboard. Keith started the engine up and pulled out of the garage.

Dean worked for a few minutes, closing up the shop. He felt a slight twinge of disappointment that he wasn't the one dropping Noelle's car off to her.

*It's okay,* he thought as he locked up the front door to the auto repair shop. *I know I'll get to see her this coming week at my PT appointment.*

He started to make his way home with his hands in his pockets, whistling slightly. Even though his body was tired and a little achy, his spirits felt strong and energized.

# CHAPTER TWELVE

Julia dug her trowel into the dirt, stabbing at the root of a dandelion. Overhead, the sky was a brilliant blue, and cotton-candy clouds drifted lazily across it. Beside Julia, Vivian was trimming dead leaves off one of her zucchini plants. The two of them had started to make a habit of spending quality time together in Vivian's garden, and it was now one of Julia's favorite things about her quiet new life away from New York.

"When did your love for growing your own vegetables start, Mom?" Julia asked, smiling at Vivian.

"Oh, when did it start?" Vivian sat back on her heels and placed her hands on her thighs, staring into space. She smiled as she thought. "I think it all started when you kids were little and your dad wanted to take you fishing. If I was inside while he was getting you ready, somehow it always turned into some kind of battle. If I made any suggestions or tried to do something differently, he would always veto my ideas. He always seemed to know better what you kids needed for the fishing trips, so I would just stay out of the way and let him get you kids ready. I knew it was his passion, and he probably did know better than me in the end because I don't go fishing. And I thought it was a nice time for you to spend with your dad."

"Huh." Julia frowned, feeling bad for her mother. Vivian was still smiling, but it struck her that her father hadn't behaved very graciously during those times. "So that's when you started gardening? To have something to do while we were gone fishing?"

"Yes." Vivian chuckled. "As soon as your father suggested a fishing trip, I'd put my gloves on and start digging out here in the tomato beds."

After a few seconds of silence, Julia asked, "Did that bother you, that Dad wanted to do it all on his own?"

Vivian shook her head. "No, it didn't. Now, if he'd acted like that all the time, that would have been different. But it was just when he was getting you four ready to go fishing. I think when I got involved he felt as though I didn't trust him to take care of you kids and get you ready. And I did, and I learned that I needed to show him that. Both parents need to know that the other trusts them."

Julia inhaled and let out a long sigh, thinking about her situation with Cooper, and feeling as though he didn't trust her to take care of Macey. Vivian immediately seemed to realize that something was on her daughter's mind.

"What are you thinking about, sweetheart?" Vivian asked, placing a hand on her daughter's arm.

"I just—well, I feel like I'm running into that issue with Cooper. I know I'm not Macey's parent, but I am his partner, and when I try to take care of her, it seems to be clear that he doesn't trust me and he'll never see me as being able to do things for Macey as well as he can. I'm trying not to be frustrated about it, but it keeps coming up, and I feel bad about it. I feel like whenever I try to take care of her, he stops me and does it his own way instead."

Vivian nodded, listening intently. "I understand

how you feel, but I don't think you need to feel too bad about it. I think it's only natural for him to act that way, since he has been raising Macey on his own for so long now."

"But what if it never changes?" Julia felt tears spring into her eyes as she voiced her fears aloud. "What if we get married someday but he never sees me as an equal parent?" She bit her lip, taking a deep breath. She wanted her future with Cooper to be a happy, comfortable one, and she wanted to be able to take care of Macey the way a mother would. She felt a surge of worry create a knot in her chest.

"Don't fret." Vivian's voice was gentle. "Thank you for sharing how you're feeling with me, but I don't think you need to worry about that at this stage. After all, you're not married, and you haven't been dating for all that long."

Julia nodded, blinking away the rest of her tears. "You're right. And I guess I can understand where he's coming from, since I've never had kids of my own. I'm not experienced in that way."

She remembered how she'd worried, when she first started dating Cooper, about how she would handle dating a man with a small child. She'd worried that she wouldn't know how to care for Macey at all. Now she felt as if she did know how to care for the little girl, but Cooper's concerns were holding her back from doing so.

"You're getting there." Vivian smiled affectionately at her daughter. "The love you have for that little girl is a great start."

"I do love her." Julia smiled, thinking about how much Macey meant to her. "She's so sweet and darling. And, I don't know, I just love her. Not just because she's so charming. There's also a protective instinct there. I just want to make sure she's okay."

Vivian nodded and squeezed Julia's hand. "Absolutely. Children need us, and we have strong instincts that encourage us to take care of them. But that being said, parenting is extremely tricky. Just because we want to take care of a child doesn't mean that we know how. I don't think anyone ever *really* knows how to be a parent. Just be patient with Cooper while he's getting used to the idea of you also caring for Macey. And maybe you should tell him how you're feeling."

"Thanks, Mom." Julia leaned over and gave her mother a sideways hug. "That's good advice."

They continued to garden, and she thought about what her mother had said. She knew that talking to her boyfriend about how she was feeling was a good idea, but she didn't feel ready to bring it up to him, at least not yet. She tried to take her mind off the troubling situation as they continued to garden, and soon the pleasant smells and the sound of the birds chirping in the trees had led her mind to other topics of thought.

# CHAPTER THIRTEEN

Hazel tapped her fingers against her lips as she looked down at the magazine that was open on the bathroom counter in front of her. There were so many different spa day ideas on the page in front of her, she hardly knew which one to look at first.

*It will depend on what supplies I have,* she thought, glancing down at all the products she had spread out on the bathroom floor. *For a foot soak, I'll need mineral salts and maybe some essential oils.*

She found the bag of Epsom salts that she'd purchased and noticed that they were lavender scented. She smiled, thinking to herself that she'd bought her supplies in such an eager hurry that she hardly remembered what she'd purchased anymore.

She looked at the other ideas on the magazine

page. There were some recipes for homemade bath bombs, but she decided against that. She wanted to have the kind of spa where she could wear silk pajamas and sit comfortably for a while. She knew she wanted to have a foot soak, and she made a mental note that she would need to get a bucket of some kind to put her feet in.

She thought to herself with a chuckle that it was a bit overwhelming, which was ironic because it was supposed to be relaxing. But she had a feeling that if she set up her spa with a lot of the different things that the magazine suggested, like candles and soothing music, it would be absolutely delightful.

"Hey, Mom?"

Hazel looked up as she heard her daughter calling for her. "I'm in here, honey! In the bathroom, looking at some stuff."

A moment later, Samantha waltzed into the bathroom and shrieked with delight when she saw all of the fun things that Hazel had spread out on the floor. "Whoa! What's all this stuff?" She crouched down, inspecting the lavender Epsom salts and the face masks and the colorful scented candles. "These look so fancy. What are you doing with them?"

"Well, I saw this magazine here when we were at the store and I got the idea to have an at-home spa day." Hazel laughed. "I thought it was time for some real self-care." She hesitated, not knowing how to explain to her daughter that she was still feeling bad that Jacob was dating someone else. She didn't know how to explain to her that she felt a need to love herself more than she usually did. "I've just been feeling a little blue lately, and I thought that having a spa day would be a fun way to pamper myself and remind myself that I can make myself feel special." As she spoke, she remembered a thought that she'd had the other day. She'd decided that she wanted to appreciate her opportunities to love the people right in front of her rather than pine over the sort of love that was absent from her life. A second later, she got an idea that made her smile. "So, I've decided to have an at-home spa day, using these supplies here and some of the ideas in this magazine. Do you want to do it with me? We could have a spa night together."

"Oh my gosh, yes!" Samantha clapped her hands together, looking thrilled. "That sounds like so much fun. I bet we'll both feel like total princesses."

"I bet we will too," Hazel said, beaming at her daughter. She suddenly felt even more excited about the spa day than she had before. "What about Thursday night? You don't have any after-school clubs then, right?"

"Nope, not on Thursdays. That sounds perfect." Samantha grinned gleefully. "So what do we do first? Looks like you want to do a foot soak, huh? We're going to need some buckets for that."

Hazel laughed. "Aye aye, Captain, you read my mind. Do we already have buckets that would work, or do we need to go out and buy some?"

"I think we've got some plastic buckets in the basement where we're storing craft supplies. We could always put the craft stuff in a box for now and use the buckets. What do you think?"

"Sounds good to me." Hazel grinned, struck by how having a teammate made her plans not feel overwhelming anymore.

"Cool, I'll go make sure they're a good size!" Samantha darted away, and Hazel turned back to the magazine with a chuckle. She turned the page, feeling excited, and then got the idea of doing her and Samantha's nails together.

*That would be so fun,* she thought eagerly. *I still have that manicure kit that Alexis gave me for Christmas. We can file our nails and use cuticle oil, and then I can help her paint hers whatever shade she wants. I have a lot of different colors, and a lot of them are sparkly, which I know she'd love.*

Hazel grinned as she started to picture all of the

fun and relaxing things that she and Samantha could do together on their spa day. She had a pencil tucked into her ponytail, and she pulled it out and started to jot down a list on the back of the magazine. She kept glancing down at the supplies that were on the bathroom floor, making sure that they had everything they needed to create her ideas.

"Here are the buckets!" Samantha appeared suddenly in the bathroom, and Hazel laughed.

"You scared me! Oh yes, those should be perfect. Great idea, honey."

"You're welcome!" Samantha set the buckets down on the floor next to the rest of the supplies with a flourish. "You know what else we need?"

"What?" Hazel pursed her lips as she looked at her daughter. She felt a surge of affection for the clever, cheerful girl who always managed to brighten her days.

"Squishy socks." Samantha nodded emphatically and disappeared again.

"Socks?" Hazel called back.

Samantha didn't reply, and Hazel chuckled and went back to making her list. Within a minute, her daughter was back, triumphantly holding up two pairs of very soft polyester socks.

"So that we can have the foot soak, put lotion on

our feet, and then put our feet in these socks."
Samantha added the socks to their stash on the
bathroom floor. "It's going to feel amazing."

Hazel laughed. "You're right. That's a brilliant
idea. You want to hear this list I've written up? You
can tell me what you think."

"Yeah!"

Hazel read her list aloud to her daughter, who
grinned as she listened.

"That all sounds great to me," Samantha said.
"What should we get ready next? How about we
pick a relaxing music playlist?"

"We could—or we could create our own?"

"Yeah! I'll go make us some popcorn. We can sit
in the living room and listen to Zen music all night."

Hazel laughed, feeling grateful that she had
someone planning with her, and that she got to bless
someone else with the fun day that she'd been
wanting to plan.

# CHAPTER FOURTEEN

Noelle parked her car in the outdoor parking lot of her apartment building and sat quietly for a moment, listening to the sound of the wind rustling in the trees around her. It was a slightly blustery but still fairly warm evening, and she was looking forward to making dinner after work and sitting out on her balcony for a while to enjoy the evening.

She tapped the steering wheel of her car affectionately before getting out. She was enjoying driving more than ever now that Dean had fixed up her car so well. She kept noticing things that he'd fixed or spruced up for free. He'd vacuumed the interior, polished the outside, and she could see by the sticker on the top left corner of her windshield that he'd changed her oil for free as well.

She opened the door to her car and got out. At that moment, a gust of wind rushed against her suddenly, causing a paper to fly out of her purse and begin to skuttle across the parking lot. She let out a short yelp and chased after it, managing to snatch it as it blew in front of her car.

As she was straightening, she noticed that her headlights were clearer than usual, and gleaming in the sunlight.

*Oh my goodness, he polished my headlights too,* she thought, letting out a giggle. *I can't believe how sweet he was about that whole thing. What a great car shop—I've never even heard of such stellar service.*

She knew though that it wasn't really the auto repair shop. It was Dean, and he'd been extra sweet to her on purpose. Maybe it was because she was his physical therapist, and he wanted to be gracious to her because she was taking the time to help him improve his osteoarthritis symptoms. Maybe it was because they were beginning to be friends. All she knew for sure was that she felt grateful to him, and seeing all the little things he'd done to her car made her feel special and happy.

She smiled as she made her way to her apartment. She thought about what a nice guy Dean was—so considerate and thoughtful, and with a sympathetic demeanor. She realized as she climbed the stairs of her building that she was excited for his upcoming physical therapy appointment. She was looking forward to seeing him and getting to talk with him again.

Once she was inside her apartment, she hung her purse up on a coat rack that was placed by the front door and made her way to the kitchen. She opened her refrigerator, wondering what she wanted to make herself for dinner.

*Something with apples,* she thought with a laugh, noticing the bag of apples that she'd purchased at a farmers market the day before. *Should I just make an apple pie after dinner, or can I create something savory using apples first?*

Smiling to herself, she sat down in a comfortable armchair near the window and began to browse Pinterest, looking for dinner recipes involving apples. She finally decided on an apple and chicken skillet, which looked mouthwatering.

She munched on one of the apples as she began to cook, since her stomach was growling and she never enjoyed cooking on an empty stomach. She turned on some cheerful, relaxing folk music and lighted a pumpkin-scented candle. Even though it felt as though autumn was just beginning to show itself, fall was one of Noelle's favorite seasons, and she was ready to embrace it wholeheartedly.

Once she had her meal simmering on the stove, she changed into soft sweatpants and a hoodie. She returned to the kitchen to check her food, and smiled when she smelled the sweet, tangy aroma that was filling the air.

She set the little table that she had out on her balcony, and when her meal was ready, she sat there to eat it. As she chewed the delicious food, she looked out across the parking lot to a line of trees that were silhouetted against the ocean. The sunset was turning the water a variety of incredible shades, and she sighed happily as she watched the waves wink and flash in the waning light.

All of a sudden, she found herself thinking about Dean. She wondered what he was doing, and if he'd gotten a chance to see the beautiful sunset. She had his number, from when he'd texted her about her car, and for a moment she considered texting him. Then she decided that would be silly—after all, they didn't know each other that well, and in a place like Rosewood Beach, it was hard not to get a chance to see the sunset.

She finished her meal and cleared the table, feeling satisfied and comfortable. It was still a beautiful evening, and she considered going back onto her balcony to read for a while.

As she was bustling around in her kitchen, cleaning up the mess she'd made while she was cooking, she heard the buzzer go off in her apartment, signaling that someone was at the front door who wanted to come upstairs to her place.

She sashayed over to the intercom and pressed the button. "Who is it?"

"It's me, sweetie, your grandmother."

"Oh, hey!" Noelle's face lit up into a smile when she heard the familiar voice of her grandmother, Gloria Calhoun. "Come right on in."

She pressed the buzzer, and less than a minute later, there was a knock on her apartment door. She opened it eagerly, revealing the gray hair and smiling face of Gloria.

"Hey, Grandma." Noelle gave her grandmother a bear hug. "What's the occasion?"

"I made a bunch of macaroons today, and I wanted to bring some to you." Gloria held up a cookie tin as they separated, her eyes bright and warm.

"Aww, Grandma!" Noelle took the tin, smiling

broadly. "You shouldn't have. You gave me that banana bread three days ago, and I just finished it." She laughed. "I'm going to be completely spoiled if you keep this up."

Gloria shook her head, her lips pursed. "I've been baking for much longer than you've been alive, and I've always shared what I made with the people I love. I'm not about to stop now. Besides, I know you love coconut macaroons."

Noelle bit her lip to suppress a fond chuckle. "You're right. Next time, how about you let me help you make them? Then I'll get some good practice in, and then the next time, I can make some for you."

"Sounds like a great deal." Gloria brushed her hands together. "Do you have any plans this evening, or can I intrude for a little while?"

"You're never an intruder." Noelle kissed her grandmother's cheek. "How about you come sit out on the balcony with me and eat some of these cookies along with some hot apple cider?"

"Oh, that sounds fantastic."

"I've got an apple theme going this evening." Noelle grinned. "I made chicken with apples for dinner."

Gloria gasped appreciatively. "Where did you find the recipe—no, never mind. I already know."

She laughed. "You found it online. You found that wonderful lemon mushroom shrimp pasta recipe online too. I'll never forget about that one—so original."

"I keep telling you to get a Pinterest, Grandma." Noelle laughed as she began to pour apple cider into a pot. "You'd love it. Or you should at least start going online a little more to look for recipes. There's so much great stuff out there."

"I can't seem to make sense of the internet." Gloria shook her head. "How about you show me some recipes on Pinterest, and then you can send me the ones that look interesting? Your grandpa knows how to print things from email. Could you email them to us?"

"I can just print them off for you here." Noelle chuckled. "Or better yet, why don't you bring over your recipe cards and we can write some down by hand together? For both of us. I like cooking from recipe cards better than squinting at my phone anyway."

"Oh, I'd love that." Gloria's face lit up. "We could watch some movies while we work."

Noelle grinned. She and her grandmother both loved old black and white movies. Watching them together was one of their favorite pastimes. "Perfect.

Let's watch some of our favorites like *The Philadelphia Story* and *Casablanca*. It's always easier to work while watching older movies like that because they're so much slower-paced than modern movies are."

"People knew how to pay attention back then." Gloria nodded.

A few minutes later, they were seated out on the balcony, sipping their hot apple cider and munching on the delicious coconut macaroons. The sun had now set, leaving only a faint flush of gold at the western edge of the horizon.

"This is delicious, thank you, sweetheart." Gloria took a sip of the hot apple cider, wiggling a little as she swallowed with relish. "Mm. Just hits the spot."

Noelle laughed at her grandmother's antics. "If we're really talking delicious, let's hear it for these cookies. I think you outdid yourself this time, Grandma."

Gloria chuckled. "Thank you, dear. I just followed the recipe. Now tell me all about how things are going at work. Do you feel like you're really settled in yet?"

"Oh, I'm getting there." Noelle took a sip of her hot apple cider. "The other physical therapist, Chip, has been really great. He's really helpful and I never feel like I can't reach out and ask him a question. And my patients have been really great. The ones that started right when I got here have been showing substantial progress, and the new ones—well, the new ones are great." She thought about Dean and found herself smiling broadly.

"Hmm, what do you mean by 'great'?" Gloria asked, cocking her head curiously.

"Uh, well, there's a very sweet old man who always brightens my day. And there's a younger man too. His name is Dean."

"Why is Dean in physical therapy?" Gloria asked. "Does he have an injury of some kind?"

"No, he has osteoarthritis." Noelle shook her head sadly. "I feel terrible for him, although I think that putting in the work of physical therapy will really get his symptoms under control."

"Oh, that's a shame. How young is he?"

Noelle wondered if it was her imagination, or if her grandmother looked slightly mischievous.

"He's... well, he's around my age. A young man. So I'm really hoping that PT will help him. He's too young to be struggling with weakness and fatigue the way he has been."

Gloria nodded. "Well, hopefully you're able to help him improve his quality of life."

"I hope so." Noelle smiled. "That's the most rewarding part of the job—when patients really start to do better. I love seeing the hope start to appear on their faces. And Dean seems like a hardworking guy, so I think he's going to put in the work and start to see progress."

"Why do you say he's hardworking? Just a hunch?"

"No." Noelle shook her head, unable to keep from smiling when she thought about Dean's auto repair shop, and all of the sweet extra things he'd done to her car. "I was having issues with my brakes on Saturday morning. Luckily Dean's shop is a three-minute drive from here, so I drove there before the issue got really serious. My brake lines had been damaged, so the brakes still worked, but I could feel that something was starting to be really off with them."

"Well, thank goodness everything worked out fine! Don't ever take chances with things like that."

"Oh, I won't. Dean told me I should get my car towed when things like the brakes start acting up. He thinks it's better to be safe than sorry and I agree with him."

"Dean's a mechanic?"

"Oh!" Noelle laughed. "I guess I'm getting ahead

of myself. Yes, he is, but he also owns Rosewood Beach's auto repair shop. And the way he took care of my car there—honestly, just the way he runs the whole place, even though I know he's been struggling with his osteoarthritis symptoms—was impressive. It's clear he cares a lot about doing a good job on things."

"That's a great quality." Gloria nodded sagely. "He sounds like a nice young man."

"Oh, he is. And while I was waiting there, I got to see some of the pictures hanging on the wall in his office. He used to be really active. He played baseball and went hiking and fishing a lot. So I'm hoping that he'll have the energy to go back to those kinds of things soon, at least some of the time."

"That's nice that you got a chance to see what it is he likes to do. It'll help you understand just how much he wants to feel better again. Not that you need motivation. I know you always give your clients your best effort."

Noelle gave her grandmother's hand a squeeze. "Thanks, Grandma. I appreciate you saying that."

They continued to munch on their cookies and sip their apple cider as their conversation wound its way toward other topics. They discussed recipes, the upcoming holidays, and Gloria encouraged Noelle to take up the habit of knitting again, because it was so relaxing.

Throughout their conversation, Noelle's thoughts kept darting back to Dean, wondering how he was doing and if PT was going to help him as much as she hoped it would.

# CHAPTER FIFTEEN

Dean stood in front of his bathroom mirror, combing his wavy hair back. It looked neat and tidy for a few seconds, and then immediately bounced back to looking tousled. He chuckled, deciding that his hair had a mind of its own, and he might as well give up on trying to make it look sleek.

He reached for his toothbrush and began to brush his teeth, glancing at the clock on the wall as he did so. He would need to leave in another five minutes if he wanted to be on time for his physical therapy appointment.

He was just about to leave the bathroom when he stopped and glanced at the cologne bottle that Alexis had given him for Christmas. It was resting on his bathroom counter, near the mirror, and for the most part, he'd only been using it as decoration, since it was a glass bottle in the shape of a car.

*I might as well try to smell extra nice for this PT appointment,* he thought. *I mean, I'm going to get all sweaty. I'm sure some cologne will help me stay smelling fresh.*

He didn't admit it to himself, but deep down he knew that he wanted to use the cologne because of Noelle. He wanted to impress her.

He left the bathroom and made his way to his bedroom, where he grabbed his wallet and tucked it into his back pocket.

"Okay," he muttered, checking his pockets. "Phone, keys, wallet. I should be good—oh, I should bring a water bottle."

Noelle had told him that the clinic provided complementary water bottles to patients that had forgotten to bring water, but she'd encouraged him to bring his own water bottle along to his appointments. He hurried into the kitchen, where he got a clean water bottle out of a cupboard and filled it with water from the refrigerator.

He paused for a moment at the back door, wondering if there was anything else he needed to remember to bring to his PT appointment. He realized that he felt jittery, almost nervous, and he shook his head at himself.

*Come on, Owens,* he thought. *It's not a big deal. You're just going to move around for a while.*

He left his house and made his way to his car. He glanced at the time on the clock once he'd started the engine and realized with a jolt that he was going to be a minute late. He grimaced as he pulled out of the driveway and made his way along the streets of Rosewood Beach. He drove carefully, but he tried to add a little speed to his drive whenever he could. He didn't want to be a minute late to his appointment, he'd been hoping to be right on time.

His efforts were rewarded, and he found himself walking into the physical therapy clinic at exactly the time that his appointment was scheduled.

The receptionist greeted him with a smile. "Welcome in, Mr. Owens. Noelle is waiting for you in her office."

"Great." He smiled, all of a sudden feeling butterflies in his chest. "Thanks."

He made his way to Noelle's office, the door of which was already ajar. He stepped through it and saw Noelle seated at her desk, wearing pink scrubs and smiling slightly as she scribbled something down in her planner. In the next moment, she looked up at him and offered him a radiant smile.

"Dean! So nice to see you." She stood up and extended her hand for a shake. He took it and shook it firmly. "Welcome in. How are you doing?"

He sat down across from her. "I'm doing well. A little tired, but not too bad today."

She nodded, jotting what he'd said down in a notebook, which he noticed had purple-lined pages. "Hopefully at the end of our session today, you'll feel more energized, but even if you feel tired, that's okay too. We want to trust the process."

He nodded, watching her hands as she wrote. She had small, gentle-looking hands, he noticed. Her fingernails were fairly short, but she'd painted them in a glossy gold color which shimmered in the light coming in through her office window and he thought they looked beautiful.

She looked up and smiled at him. "And before we even get started on official business, I wanted to thank you for the excellent work you did on my car. It's running great, and I've been noticing all the extra things you did for me, like vacuuming and polishing the headlights. It was really very kind of you, and I wanted to express my gratitude."

"Oh, don't mention it." Dean could feel heat

creeping up his neck, but he smiled through the way he was suddenly feeling flustered. "I just wanted to make sure you felt welcome here in town. I remember you said you haven't been here for all that long."

She smiled warmly at him. "Well, it was very thoughtful. I'm going to recommend your place to everyone I know. I'll be sure to spread your name around town."

He laughed. "To be honest, most people here probably already know about me. There are advantages to being the only mechanic shop in town."

She shook her head, smiling. "Then I'll tell all my friends from out of town to bring their cars here too—even the ones who live on the other side of the country."

"If you do that, I'll be so busy, I won't have time for PT. I'm sure you have a lot of friends."

For a moment, they sat there grinning at each other, both of them laughing slightly.

"How did your excursion on Saturday go?" he asked her. "Do you feel like you got to see all of Rosewood Beach's many attractions?"

She shook her head. "Oh, hardly. I mean, I saw a great deal of them, but I barely walked through a quarter of the town. I got really sidetracked in the parks. I love nature, so I paused to look at all of the details there, if you know what I mean."

"Oh, I do, for sure. I also love hiking. There's so many things to pay attention to. Sometimes hikes are about the exercise, and sometimes they're about slowing down to notice all of the amazing things that nature has to offer. Like different kinds of leaves and insects."

"I agree. Usually, we go through life at too quick of a pace to stop and really appreciate the things around us."

She was looking at him with a warmth in her eyes that he liked very much.

"You know, if you want, I could show you around town." He cleared his throat slightly. "I've lived here all my life, so I know all the good places to see. What do you say?" All he could think about was how easy she was to talk to, and how he wanted more opportunities to talk with her. Besides, showing her around town seemed like the neighborly thing to do.

"Really?" Her face lit up. "I would love that. It would be so fun to get a tour of Rosewood Beach from an expert."

He grinned. "Great." He felt a flurry of

excitement over the fact that she'd said yes. "What day of the week might work well for you?"

"I have off on Friday. Would that work with your schedule?"

He nodded. "I own the shop, so I make the schedule. It'll be easy for me to make that my day off as well."

"Perfect." She turned to her computer and began to type rapidly.

"Are you putting it down in your schedule?" he asked, chuckling slightly.

She shook her head. "No, I'm checking the weather. Ah! Should be a beautiful day that day. Sunny, slightly cool. Perfect jacket weather."

"Well, fantastic." He found himself grinning at her, and he noticed that she was wearing a pair of gold earrings that had small diamond studs on the sides. She seemed to have applied a little more makeup than usual, and in the next moment, he realized that she'd applied a rich perfume, just as he'd put on cologne.

His heart rate picked up a little as he wondered if she'd done those things because she knew that she was going to see him that day.

*Oh, come on, Dean,* he told himself, trying his best to brush those thoughts aside. *Don't flatter yourself so much. She probably just felt like dressing up a little bit today—or maybe she has an event right after work.*

Even so, he couldn't help admiring her earrings and appreciating the lovely way she smelled.

"Well, now that we have that plan all good and settled, I guess it's time to get to the real reason why you're here." Noelle smiled, standing up. "You ready for some physical therapy?"

He liked the energetic, cheerful way in which she spoke. It helped him feel less nervous about how the physical therapy might make him feel.

"Sounds great." He stood up, smiling back at her. Even though he felt a little trepidatious about physical therapy, he didn't feel trepidatious at all about the day that the two of them had planned on Friday.

# CHAPTER SIXTEEN

Alexis was barely aware of the sounds of The Lighthouse Grill that were humming around her. She was sitting at a booth in the back of the pub, alongside a window that offered a breathtaking view of the ocean. A half-finished tuna melt with sweet potato fries was on the table at her elbow, but her attention was on something else besides her food.

It was her lunch break, and ever since she'd arrived at work that day, she'd been itching to open the fanny pack that she'd brought along with her and take out the things inside it. Those things were plastic strings, beads, and other tools that she needed to make a bracelet. She'd had the idea for a beautiful bracelet the previous evening as she'd been falling asleep, and ever since she'd been impatient to test out her idea.

She exhaled in a happy sigh as she gazed down at the progress she'd already made. For the bracelet, she was weaving three different strands of beads together in a lovely, whimsical pattern.

*This was such a good idea to bring my jewelry-making supplies along with me to the pub*, she thought as her fingers worked busily. *I feel like I'm not even at work right now. This is so much fun.*

She always enjoyed her waitressing shifts, unless she was particularly tired for some reason, but making jewelry was a whole new level of enjoyment for her. She felt both calm and uplifted, and although she had the patience to work carefully, she felt eager to see the finished product of her creation.

She glanced at her watch, noting that her lunch break was almost half over. She took another bite of her tuna melt, wiped off her fingers carefully, and then went back to work. In a few minutes, her bracelet was done, and she held it up to the light, feeling a surge of satisfaction.

She ate a little more of her food, and then started on another bracelet. Now that she was familiar with the pattern, she was able to join the beads and string them together much more quickly. In a few minutes, she'd finished a second bracelet and was moving on to her third.

All at once, she heard someone cough gently. She looked up, startled, and gasped softly when she saw her husband Grayson leaning against the side of the booth, smiling down at her.

"Grayson!" She laughed, surprised and pleasantly flustered. "I've been so wrapped up in my own world here, I had no idea you were there."

"That's okay." He grinned at her. "I liked watching you work."

She felt herself blushing. "How long have you been watching me?"

He glanced at his watch. "Oh, about four minutes."

She threw her head back, laughing. "Well, either I'm just so comfortable with you that I'm able to not even notice when you're watching me, or I was so engrossed in this work that I was blind to everything else."

"I'd like to think it's a combination of both." He winked at her. "You were clearly engrossed in that work—you have the focus of a true professional—and I hope you're comfortable around me. I am your husband, after all."

She grinned at him. "Well, I know for sure that

I'm very comfortable around you." She picked up the fanny pack and her purse, which were resting on the seat next to her, and moved them to the other side of her so that he could sit down. "Why don't you sit down here and help me finish these sweet potato fries?"

"Sure." He sat down and gave her an affectionate peck on the lips. "You're so nice to me. I startle you and then you let me sit next to you anyway."

She laughed. "It was a surprise. A very pleasant surprise."

"I was thinking that maybe we could eat together, but the table looks pretty full already."

"Oh, we still can. I'm only half done with my food, and you know I eat twice as slowly as you anyway."

"Well, okay, but I don't think there's room on this table for anything else." He gestured to all of her jewelry-making supplies with a smile.

"I was just having some fun," she said, laughing a little. "It's not like I need to finish this project right now." She swept her beads and strings and her half-finished bracelet into the fanny pack. She left the two finished bracelets on the table, and Grayson picked one of them up eagerly.

"This looks fantastic, Alexis," he said, gazing at it admiringly. "You made this?"

"I did." She nodded, her stomach fluttering. His praise made her happy. "You really think it's good?"

"It's more than good. It's skillfully made and originally designed. I remember how you used to make jewelry sometimes when we were living in L.A. You said once that it was your favorite hobby, and I could always see that. You always have so much joy on your face when you're making jewelry."

"I do?" She watched his face, noticing how proud of her he looked. Her heart stirred with gratitude that she had such a supportive husband. "I do really love it, but in these past few years I kind of forgot all about it. I didn't forget how to make jewelry though." She gestured to the bracelets she'd made. "It's like riding a bike. My fingers remember what they're doing as much as my brain still understands how to do it."

"I think it's more than that." He turned the bracelet over in his hand, examining it closely. "Look at how you've managed to weave these different strands of beads together without exposing the string underneath, even when you make the strands turn at a sharp angle. It's really well done. This is some genuinely impressive craftsmanship. And I'm not a woman, but I bet if we went out onto the sidewalk right now and showed this to all the women passing by, they would all tell you it's absolutely gorgeous."

She laughed. "Why can't you just tell me it's absolutely gorgeous?"

He shook his head ruefully. "Because I have no instinct for these things, so you can't trust my word for it." Warmth filled his expression as he added, "Besides, the only absolutely gorgeous thing in my eyes is you."

She blew him a kiss, feeling her heart stir with joy at his compliment. "Well, thank you, but this is just for fun. I have some skill, I guess, but I'm an amateur. I'll probably give everyone bracelets for Christmas or something as a way of getting rid of all the jewelry I just know I'm going to end up making."

He shook his head, looking into her eyes.

"What, no bracelets for Christmas?" she teased. "You don't want one?"

"I mean, go ahead and give out jewelry for Christmas if you want to. I'm sure everyone would be thrilled to get something you made as a gift. But I'm serious." He reached across the table and took her hand in his. "I've been noticing that you seemed a bit melancholy lately, as if you felt like something was missing. And I've been wondering how I can help you stop feeling that way, but it looks like you've reached a solution all by yourself."

She squeezed his hand. "Thank you. I appreciate you looking out for me. You're right, I have been feeling kind of restless. I realized it was because I missed having a creative outlet, and I think this hobby will be just the thing. I'm enjoying myself so much."

"I think this can be more than a hobby, Alexis."

For a few seconds, she blinked at her husband, not quite processing what he was saying. "What do you mean?" she asked finally.

"I think it's really important for a person to have a job that they love."

"But this is just a hobby, Grayson—I can't sell my bracelets. I mean, at least not enough of them to make a living."

"Maybe not a full living, not enough to cover a mortgage and cars and food and everything, but I think that your jewelry could bring in an income. And you'd be really happy doing it, and that's what's most important, I think. It's better to have a job you love and less money than do a job you hate and be rolling in wealth. Trust me, I know."

He made a playful grimace, referring to the

extremely lucrative company he'd run before moving to Rosewood Beach to repair his relationship with Alexis.

"I was so busy and stressed that I wasn't appreciating the truly good things in my life at all," he continued. "Like my wife. I'm much happier here making less money and having the time to spend with you and do things that I truly enjoy."

She smiled at him. "I'm so proud of you for making that decision. I was so afraid I was going to lose you back then. Our life together now feels like a dream come true."

"And I think it can feel even more like a dream come true. What do you say to trying to turn your hobby into a job?"

"I—I don't know," she stammered. "I mean, it sounds incredible, but I don't want to get my hopes up."

"I understand, but all great accomplishments require risk. How about you let me show you what your options are? I can create a list of business strategies to show you the possibilities. How does that sound?"

She found herself laughing, both from joy and a kind of delighted amusement that her husband, the successful businessman, was so ready to take her little bracelets and turn them into a full-blown business operation. "Okay. Yes. Thank you, sweetheart."

"Of course." He leaned forward for a kiss, and instead she fed him one of the sweet potato fries. "Mmpf. Delicious, but I'd rather have a kiss."

"You can have that too." She leaned forward and gave him an affectionate peck on the lips.

A waitress came by, and Grayson ordered a cup of soup and another tuna melt. He and Alexis ate together for the remainder of her lunch break, beginning to discuss the details of what a jewelry making business might look like.

She felt her excitement growing as they talked about it. In many ways, the whole concept seemed too good to be true, but Grayson seemed to think that it was more than plausible.

*He's being so sweet, but I don't think anything will come of this,* she thought. *But even if it doesn't, I feel so blessed that Grayson noticed that I was feeling down and that he cares this much. He's a good partner in so many different ways.*

When Alexis's lunch break was over, she left the booth, but Grayson stayed to finish his meal. As she started to take care of other tables in the dining room, she kept glancing at her husband as she worked. Often, he was looking at her too, and they'd share a smile. But sometimes, she saw him sitting there staring at the bracelets that she'd made with a proud expression on his face.

# CHAPTER SEVENTEEN

Hazel tucked the last dinner plate into the sink and turned to her daughter with a smile. "Are you ready?"

"Yes!"

It was the evening that they'd planned to have their spa day on, and both Hazel and Samantha were bubbly with excitement. They'd made sure they had everything ready to go the day before, and they'd just finished up a quick and delicious dinner of homemade barbeque chicken pizza.

"What's the first step?" Samantha asked as she put a jug of chocolate milk back into the refrigerator.

"The first step is putting on our silky pajamas and robes."

The day before, they'd gone to the store and

picked out matching sets of pink silky pajamas and robes. Samantha had said they looked like princess pajamas, and they reminded Hazel of the kinds of things that movie stars wore in old black and white films.

The two of them scampered upstairs to their bedrooms to get ready. Hazel changed into her soft, slippery pajamas and put on the robe, tying the sash gently around her waist. She pulled her hair back into a messy bun so that it wouldn't get in her way when they were putting on their face masks.

"There," she said to her reflection with a grin. "You look like you're ready for some relaxation."

She left her bedroom and found Samantha waiting for her in the hallway, bouncing up and down like a jackrabbit with excitement.

"Oh, you're adorable!" Hazel cooed, giving her daughter a hug. "Before we do anything else, we should take a selfie."

They posed in the upstairs hallway for a few selfies, and Hazel made a mental note to send the pictures to her sisters later. She knew they'd love to see them. But for the rest of the night, she knew that true relaxing involved turning her phone off. She turned off her cell phone and tucked it inside a little bookshelf that was nestled against a wall in the upstairs hallway.

"There," she said, sighing with satisfaction. "Let's go look at the next thing on our list."

They'd written up an agenda for the evening, mostly for fun, but also because Hazel had read once that planning things in detail could make them more relaxing so that there wasn't any decision-making stress involved.

They went back downstairs to the living room, where they'd already set up their foot soak buckets, manicure supplies, and face masks. The coffee table was absolutely covered in girly products, and Hazel thought to herself cheerfully that it had never looked better.

"Okay," Samantha said, reading the list they'd made. "First thing is face masks and foot soaks. Well, actually the next thing is turning on our spa music playlist."

Hazel did the honors, going over to her laptop and turning on the spa music playlist they'd made. She also turned on the TV and pulled up a video of a crackling fireplace mixed with the sounds of a windy rainstorm.

"Oh, I love that." Samantha grinned. "Okay, then after foot soaks and face masks, we put lotion on our feet and put the socks on, and we give each other shoulder massages, and then it's manicures and pedicures."

"Sounds perfect." Hazel smiled at her daughter, feeling more relaxed already. "Oh! We almost forgot the candles."

They went around the living room, carefully lighting a collection of scented and unscented candles. They'd carefully chosen which candles to use, making sure that the scents would blend well together. There was lavender, eucalyptus, peppermint, and sandalwood, and soon the room smelled absolutely incredible.

The last thing left to do was prepare the hot water for their foot soaks. Once that was done, Hazel poured it into the buckets and tested the temperature, making sure that it was hot enough to be relaxing without being uncomfortable. Next, they poured the lavender scented Epsom salts into the foot soak buckets, and the room was immediately filled with the rich, relaxing aroma of lavender.

"Oh, this is nice." Hazel sighed, amazed that her homey little living room could be transformed into such a relaxing paradise. "Good job, honey."

"Good job to you too!" Samantha was sitting

down on the couch and sliding her feet into her foot soak. "It was your idea."

Hazel sat down next to her daughter and slipped her feet into the hot water of her foot soak. She sighed involuntarily, feeling tension she didn't even know she had leaving her body immediately.

Samantha made some kind of happy murmuring noise beside her, but for the next few minutes, they were both quiet, listening to the relaxing sounds that filled the room, feeling the hot water of the foot soaks on their tired feet, and smelling the wonderful, calming aromas that filled the room.

"Hey."

Hazel opened her eyes, feeling Samantha tap her arm gently.

"What is it, honey?" she asked, feeling almost as if she was being roused from a nap.

"Face masks," Samantha said, holding up a couple of shimmery plastic packets.

"Right." Hazel nodded. "Good call, we almost forgot about those."

They unwrapped their face masks and placed them gently on their faces. The cool, moisturizing mask felt incredible on Hazel's skin. She adjusted it carefully, smoothing the damp fabric across her face, and then sat back, feeling a wave of contentment.

She closed her eyes again, thinking to herself that she was starting to feel the stress that she'd been carrying ever since finding out that Jacob had a girlfriend begin to melt away.

After a few more minutes of relaxing in silence, she and Samantha began to talk. They giggled over a story that Vivian had told them the other day of something Julia had done as a little girl, and they discussed things that they wanted to bake together.

"How's school going?" Hazel asked after a while.

"Oh, school is great. Sometimes I feel tired and I'd rather be doing something else, but I like being there with my friends. And we're learning a lot of interesting stuff."

"You're still doing really well, according to your teacher. I'm really proud of you."

"Thanks, Mom."

Samantha's smile looked funny through her face mask, and it made Hazel laugh, and then Samantha started laughing too.

When their attack of giggles was over, Samantha said, "And I'm really excited about the school dance. I've never been to one before. Everyone talks about it almost every day."

"Oh, I remember school dances." Hazel smiled, feeling a surge of nostalgia. "You get to wear a pretty dress and all your friends are there. We always thought the decorations were so cool—there's usually a lot of color and sparkly things. It's so much fun to listen to the music and dance. And you start to feel a little more like an adult, I guess. I remember that being really exciting when I was your age."

As soon as the words left her mouth, Hazel felt a pang of sadness. She didn't feel ready for Samantha to be growing up. Her little girl was still so young and innocent, and she thought about all of the big girl problems that Samantha would have to be facing soon. She didn't want her daughter to have to deal with the struggles that came with growing up.

*There are a lot of joys involved in growing up too,* she reminded herself. *It's not as though it's all bad.*

Still, she felt a sudden cloud of worry for a moment. Then she brushed those thoughts aside, reminding herself to focus on the present and enjoy the time that she was spending with her daughter right then and there.

"I'm so excited." Samantha wiggled a little, looking up at the ceiling as if she was seeing other things in her imagination. "The theme for the dance is *The Wizard of Oz*, so there's going to be a yellow brick road in the gym, and they're going to make one of the back walls look like the Emerald City. All green and sparkly. We're going to take so many pictures." She laughed.

"That sounds like fun! Do you know what kind of dress you want to wear? Do you want to try to match the theme?"

"Oh, I do. Willow is wearing a black dress and red shoes and she's going to give herself green eyeshadow, so she kind of looks like the Wicked Witch of the West. Oh! And she's going to wear striped stockings with her dress. It's going to be awesome. And then—"

"She's wearing makeup?" Hazel hesitated. She'd told Samantha that she didn't want her to wear makeup until she was older, because she didn't want her to be too preoccupied with her appearance.

She wondered if Samantha would ask to wear makeup to the dance, and what she should say if she was asked for permission. Hazel thought that maybe a special occasion like that would be an okay time to wear makeup, especially if her friends were already doing it. She didn't want Samantha to feel left out. Then again, what if all of her friends started having bad habits? Then Samantha would have to feel left out, because Hazel would never agree to certain kinds of things—

"Mom?"

"What?" Hazel turned back to Samantha, shaking her head as if that could clear away all of the thoughts that had suddenly swarmed her. "Sorry, honey."

"You totally checked out for a second. I said, 'Yes, she's wearing eyeshadow, but I don't want to wear any makeup.' Maybe paint some glitter on my face, but I don't want to try to wear lipstick or anything like that."

"Oh." Hazel smiled at her daughter, feeling relieved. "Sounds great. I'd love to help you put glitter on your face."

"Thank you! That goes with my theme. See, Willow is going as the Wicked Witch of the West, so then I thought that I could go as Glinda, that good witch who shows up at the beginning of the movie in a pink bubble and she's all smiley and stuff."

"I remember. That sounds like an awesome idea. You're going to make an adorable Glinda."

"Thanks, Mom. I have my dress all picked out. Well, I have four different dresses picked out, and I just have to decide between them."

"What if one of them is gone before you decide?"

Samantha shook her head, grinning. "No, Mom, they're all online."

"Oh. Right." Hazel nodded as Samantha got her

cell phone out of her pocket and started to pull up pictures of dresses. Mother and daughter leaned in close together to look at the phone screen and admire the dresses.

All four of the dresses were pink, and two of them had fluffy tulle skirts. Hazel found herself captivated by the sight of the dresses, and she remembered how fun it had been to look for fancy dresses like that—although she had done all her shopping in person.

"Oh, those are all so cute. Honestly. I don't know how you're going to pick one."

"I know!" Samantha sighed happily. "A good problem to have, I guess. Which one would you pick, if you had to decide between all four?"

"Oh, gosh." Hazel leaned in toward Samantha's phone, looking at the pictures as Samantha scrolled back and forth between them. "I think... if I absolutely had to decide..."

Samantha realized that her mother was pausing for dramatic effect and laughed. "Come on, Mom! Which one?"

"I think this one." Hazel tapped the dress that Samantha had on the screen at that moment. "I love the tulle skirt with the glitter in it. Not a lot of social engagements allow for you to show up looking sparkly, so I say go for it."

"I'm going to get glitter everywhere though, aren't I?"

"Well, of course. That's because you're magical." Hazel booped Samantha's nose gently with her fingertip. "And I don't mind you getting a little glitter in our house—and I'm sure there will be plenty of glitter at that dance anyway. I'm so excited for you! You're going to have such a great time going with Willow."

Samantha smiled, but Hazel could see right away that her daughter was about to throw a plot twist her way. Samantha's eyes were suddenly dancing with excitement. She hesitated for a moment and then spoke slowly.

"Well, actually, even though Willow and I are planning our outfits around each other, I'm hoping to go with someone else. You know, like officially go with someone."

There were a few seconds of silence as Hazel started to process her daughter's words. "You mean... as in, you want to go with a boy?"

Samantha's giggles confirmed that before the almost-teenager spoke. "Yeah. I mean, I don't know if he's going to ask me or not, but I've been really hoping."

Hazel felt her heart rate pick up. Of all the things connected to Samantha growing up that made her nervous, this was by far the most nerve-wracking one. She immediately felt a flush of worry, and her mind began to race, wondering how old this boy was and if he was a good person or someone selfish and inconsiderate.

She tried to remain calm as she cleared her throat. "A boy, huh? What's his name?"

"His name is Austin," Samantha said, and it was clear from her swooning tone that she had more than just a little crush on him. "He's so cute, Mom. I've had a crush on him ever since the first time I saw him in literature class. He's got this wavy blond hair. He kind of looks like a movie star. And he's got the best laugh. Like, he'll be talking with his friends and then all of a sudden everyone in the room can hear this amazing laugh. Usually it's kind of obnoxious when people laugh really loudly, but it isn't when he does it. His laugh sounds really nice. He just kind of brightens up the whole room."

"He sounds like a nice guy." Hazel did her best to smile. "Is he? I mean, does he seem like a nice person?"

"Oh, so nice. He's got a dog and he's been training it really carefully. I've heard him telling his friends about it. And he's got a little sister who he babysits. Sometimes I've seen her run out of the car to hug him when we're all getting picked up at school."

"That's great." Hazel cleared her throat again, still trying to get her heart rate to go back down. "He sounds nice."

"Oh, he's more than nice. He's wonderful."

For a few moments, neither of them said anything. Samantha looked as though she was lost in some kind of happy daydream, and Hazel felt as though she was having a bad dream. She'd known that Samantha would start to like boys and want to go on dates at some point, but she'd never heard her daughter mention boys before. She hadn't had any idea that Samantha was starting to feel those kinds of things already.

*It'll be fine,* Hazel told herself firmly. *This is just a part of life. He seems like a nice boy. But—*

Her heart twisted as she imagined Samantha having to watch as Austin developed a crush on some other girl and started dating her instead. Then she shook herself. They were still too young to date, she didn't need to worry about that. But she could tell that Samantha had really gotten her hopes up about the dance.

There were a lot of girls in Samantha's school, and it was more than possible that Austin wouldn't ask Samantha to the dance. He might not ask anyone at all, or he very well could ask another girl and Samantha would get hurt.

"Tell me about when you went to your first dance, Mom," Samantha said, turning to her mother with a grin. "Was it fun? Who did you go with?"

"Oh my," Hazel tried to shake the cobwebs of worry from her brain. "Yes, I remember it being very fun. I went dress shopping with my sisters and they helped me pick out a dress. It was pale blue with a skirt that spun out amazingly when I twirled. I put it on a whole hour before the dance started so that I could stand in the living room and just twirl around." She laughed a little at the memory.

"Did you go with somebody?"

"Did I? I don't even remember—I don't think we were really going with people at that age."

She thought about her first dance, trying to recall, and then she remembered that she had wanted to go with someone. She'd wanted to go with Jacob, and he'd gone with one of the other girls.

She swallowed, not wanting to think about how long ago her crush on Jacob had started.

"Hmm. Going dress shopping does sound fun." Samantha sounded eager. "Maybe we can use these dresses I picked out as inspiration but go shopping in person. Maybe we could get Grandma and Aunt Julia and Aunt Alexis to come with us."

"That sounds like a lot of fun." Hazel smiled at her daughter, genuinely excited about the prospect of getting to go dress shopping with her and the other women in the Owens family. "I'll call all of them later tonight and see when they're free. Friday's probably a good day, yeah?"

"Works for me," Samantha said cheerfully.

"Okay, great." Hazel leaned over and kissed Samantha on the side of the head. They went back to being quiet, but Hazel no longer felt relaxed and peaceful.

She was remembering how much she'd liked Jacob, even at Samantha's age. Her crush on him had felt like some *Romeo and Juliet* fantasy, and she'd hoped that he would someday walk up to her and ask her on a date or tell her he liked her and was interested in her. She sat with her eyes closed, beginning to remember all kinds of things, even an old dream she'd had once in which he'd given her a bouquet of roses in front of the whole school.

After a while, she'd stopped liking him so much and moved on to other crushes—but it was only after he'd started dating other girls and she'd cried herself to sleep a couple of times. She felt a rising panic, worrying that Samantha was going to end up feeling hurt in the same way. Jacob had seemed so wonderful, just like Austin seemed wonderful to Samantha, and even though Jacob had never done anything to hurt her, she'd felt so let down when he wasn't interested in her. And here she was, years later, feeling the same way again.

And then, after Jacob, Hazel had fallen in love with and married Samantha's father, who had turned out to be unreliable and uncaring. Hazel never wanted her baby daughter to have to go through something like that.

Feeling restless, she opened her eyes and looked at the time. "I think it's time to take our face masks off, honey," she said, feeling relieved to have something to do. "Then we can moisturize our feet and start doing our manicures."

"Ooh, yes please!" Samantha sat up eagerly, ready for the next part of their spa night.

Hazel smiled at her, telling herself firmly that she was going to put aside her worries for the rest of the night. She needed some time to process, so she could figure out how to handle this new era of life. Thinking about it any more that night was just going to freak her out, and that would be a shame, since relaxation was the goal of the evening.

"Perfect. What color do you want to paint your nails?"

"I want that pink color," Samantha said, pointing to a hot pink nail polish bottle. "It's such a happy color."

Hazel chuckled. "You're right. It's a very happy color."

They continued to enjoy their spa night together as they painted their nails and chatted. After a while, Hazel's nervousness melted away and she found herself enjoying the evening again. Samantha was always fun company, and Hazel's body was responding well to the way she was pampering it. She knew that soon, she would need to face her fears about Samantha being interested in boys, but for the time being, she just got to have a fun, relaxing night with her daughter.

\* \* \*

Dean leaned back in his armchair, letting out a long yawn. He stretched, pleased to find that his body felt more loose and relaxed than usual. It was clear that physical therapy was starting to help him already, and that gave him a sense of hope like he hadn't had in a while.

He set down his book on a little table resting next to the armchair and glanced at his watch. It was almost nine p.m., and he was getting sleepy.

*I'm an adult,* he thought with a chuckle. *I can go to bed whenever I want. Time to go to bed.*

He stood up and wandered into the kitchen, where he poured himself a glass of milk and turned out the lights. He carried the milk upstairs with him along with his book, his mind going over the events of his day. It had been a good day, productive and pleasant. Best of all, he'd had more energy than he'd had in a while, and even though he was feeling tired and sleepy at the moment, he was relishing the fact that his symptoms were improving.

He sat in bed for a while, reading more of his book and slowly sipping his glass of milk. Outside, the night was turning blustery, and he wondered if an autumn storm was on its way. He glanced out the window a few times, enjoying the sight of a brilliantly silver moon shining through the tree branches.

Finally, he got back out of bed and went into the bathroom to brush his teeth. By that point, he was so sleepy that his eyelids were drooping, and he could feel that all his limbs were heavy with drowsiness. He was just making his way back into his bedroom when his phone began to ring.

He picked it up from where it was resting on the end of his bed and saw that the caller was one of his friends who he'd met at a car show several years before. They shared a love for car restoration and often swapped advice and tips on where to find hard to locate parts. He answered the phone eagerly, suddenly feeling more awake.

"Hey, Shawn!" Dean found himself grinning. "How's it going?"

"Dean, my man! It's been too long. How have you been holding up?"

They spent a few minutes catching up, but Dean found himself holding back from sharing the news of his diagnosis. He didn't want Shawn to feel bad for him, and he wanted their conversation to be about the positive things that were going on in their lives.

"So the reason why I'm calling—"

"Yeah, at this hour?" Dean's tone was playful. "It's time for bed. I'm in my pajamas here. You could have woken me up."

Shawn's big booming laugh practically made the phone vibrate. "You're getting boring, huh? Wow."

"Oh, yeah. I even drank of glass of milk while reading first."

"I'm going to have to save you from yourself. Luckily, I have just the thing to make you feel less boring. I've got a 1980's Mustang on my hands, and I just don't have the time to fix her up. What do you say? Are you up for the challenge?"

"Oh, man." Dean felt his heart stir with excitement. He loved Mustangs, and he'd been wanting to get his hands on an older one for a while. "That sounds amazing, Shawn, it really does, but I—"

"Oh, come on, Dean. It's free. I'm just handing you pure gold here."

Dean scratched the back of his neck, feeling a tug toward the idea of fixing up the car. In the past, he would have leapt at such an opportunity without hesitation, but now he was struggling to make a decision. It was something he wanted, there was no doubt about that, but he wasn't sure if he would have the energy for it. What if he tried working on the car, and realized that it was too much for him? He felt sure that he would feel even more disappointed about not having the energy to fix it if it was actually there with him instead of miles away.

"Well, Shawn, I'd love to, you know I would. And I appreciate you calling me and offering it to me. But I've been running into some health issues and I've had to take it easy lately."

"Oh, I'm sorry to hear that. Are you okay?"

"Yeah, I'm okay. Nothing terminal or anything like that. Just a lot of fatigue and soreness."

"Well, don't let that stop you from living your best life. I mean, take care of yourself and everything, but they say that doing things that bring you joy is good for your body. Why don't you take a look at the Mustang and see what you think? It's not like you'd have a deadline to finish it up. Heck, take ten years to do it, who cares? You wouldn't have to work on it right away, and you could do it slowly once you do start."

Dean found himself smiling, suddenly filled with eagerness. He realized that Shawn was right, and that taking a look at the car would be the most logical path forward. Besides, Shawn was a good friend of his, and Dean wanted to show him his gratitude by being willing to come and look at the car that Shawn was offering. "Okay, you got me. Those are some good points. I'll take a look at it."

"I knew you wouldn't be able to turn it down!" Shawn crowed. "You're too much of a car buff."

"Well, yes, and Ford Mustangs are especially near and dear to my heart." Dean couldn't help grinning. "Thanks again for offering, I really appreciate it."

"Of course! I can't wait to see the look on your face when you see her. I know you're going to decide to take the car. She's really a beauty."

The two friends chatted for a while longer, catching up about the details of their lives and planning a time for Dean to go see the Mustang. As they hung up and Dean climbed back into bed, he felt a sense of eagerness that he hadn't felt in a while. He felt proud of himself for choosing to be optimistic about being able to go back to his hobbies. It was more than possible that with the help from Noelle's PT guidance, his energy levels would become good enough to allow him to work on the car in his spare time.

As he turned out the light and laid his head down on the pillow, he felt his heart stir with anticipation. He felt grateful that Shawn had reached out and grateful that he had an opportunity to work on one of his favorite hobbies again. Maybe what Shawn had said was true—maybe the joy that it brought him would be good for him in more ways than one.

# CHAPTER EIGHTEEN

Noelle stepped back from her mirror, inspecting her reflection with a smile. She'd pulled her hair back into a becoming French braid, and her cheeks were flushed with both applied blush and a natural glow. It was Friday morning, the day that Dean was going to show her around Rosewood Beach, and she couldn't have been more excited.

Rather than put on another hiking-inspired outfit like the one she'd worn the last time she went exploring around town, she'd decided to wear something a little more chic. She'd chosen a pretty sage green jumpsuit and a pair of white Keds. She'd added gold stud earrings and a delicate gold bracelet to her wrist, making the look feel complete. She told herself that she just felt like dressing up for her fun day off, and that the fact that she'd put more care into her appearance than usual had nothing to do with Dean.

She spun around once, just for fun. She felt almost giddy with excitement, and once she'd finished twirling, she sighed contentedly. She scampered over to her phone to check to see if Dean had texted her, and sure enough he had.

**DEAN: Hey! Good morning. Want to meet up at the gazebo in the town square at 10:30?**

She wasted no time in typing out a reply.

**NOELLE: Yes! Sounds great. See you soon!**

She smiled and tucked her phone into her pocket. She went through a mental checklist, making sure she had everything she needed for the day in her small over-the-shoulder white leather bag that she'd decided to pair with her outfit. She had a small water bottle, her usual packet of first-aid items, her wallet, and a pair of sunglasses.

*And I already applied sunscreen,* she thought. *I hope Dean applied sunscreen.*

She glanced down at her phone screen,

considering texting him to remind him. Then she laughed and told herself that wasn't her place. He was a grown man; it was up to him if he decided to put on sunscreen or not.

She slung her purse over her shoulder and made her way out of her apartment. It was a gorgeous day outside, a little crisp, but sunny enough to be warm and pleasant. She got into her car and drove the short distance to the town square, her anticipation mounting as she got closer.

She had no idea where Dean was planning on taking her that day, but she wasn't worried. She knew that whatever he had planned was going to be wonderful. She trusted him completely, and there was something about him that drew her to him, making her feel confident in his ability to take care of her.

She found a shady parking spot under a crabapple tree and parked there. Her eyes scanned the town square eagerly, wondering if she would be able to see Dean walking up to the gazebo. She didn't seem him, but a quick glance at her watch told her that she was a little less than ten minutes early.

She set off across the town square, admiring the landscaping that was still beautiful even after most of the flowers had faded for the season. There was a brilliancy to the hue of blue that covered the sky, and the sunlight dappled the lawn of the town square in beautiful patterns cast by the trees.

As she reached the gazebo, she found herself grinning. Dean was already there, sitting on a bench under the roof of the gazebo. He was facing the other way, and his back was turned to her, but she found herself admiring the way he looked even though she couldn't see his face. He was wearing a dark blue leather jacket, and his windswept hair looked endearingly tousled.

"Dean!"

He turned around, and his face lit up into a smile when he saw her. "Hey, Noelle! Thanks for meeting me here."

"Are you kidding? You're the one I should be thanking. It's so sweet of you to give me a tour like this."

"You're welcome." His eyes gleamed with an almost tender light. "I'm happy to do it. Rosewood Beach is a great town to explore, and well—you're not bad company."

She found herself flushing slightly under his compliment. Before she could think of anything to say in response, he handed her a coffee.

"Here, I brought this for you," he said. "It's from Seaside Sweets Bakery. It's their signature drink."

"What is it?" she asked curiously, sniffing the opening of the coffee cup. A rich, minty aroma wafted up at her. She noticed that Dean was holding a coffee cup identical to hers.

"They call it 'The Grasshopper' but don't let that name throw you off." He laughed. "It's my favorite drink they have there. It's a dark chocolate mocha with peppermint flavoring. And, as you'll notice once you take a sip, they add peppermint sprinkles on top of the whipped cream. It's really delicious."

"Oh, gosh." Noelle eagerly took a sip and was floored by the taste. "Dean, that's fantastic! Thank you for bringing this to me. That was really thoughtful of you." She smiled shyly at him, not knowing what else to say. She felt touched that he had gone out of his way yet again to be kind to her.

"I did even better than that." He picked up a white paper bag that was resting on the bench behind him and slipped his hand inside it. From it he pulled a plump doughnut dusted in cinnamon sugar. "I also brought both of us churro doughnuts. Seaside Sweets Bakery is one of the best places in town, and I wanted to share some of my favorite menu items with you."

"But... I mean, I could have met you there." She took the doughnut from him, noticing how fluffy and mouthwatering it looked. "And then I could have paid for my own treats. You didn't need to buy these for me."

Dean shrugged; his eyes filled with a boyish light. "It's not a problem. Besides, I wanted us to be able to get going right away. There's a lot to see."

"So much to see that we can't sit here for a little while and eat these doughnuts?" She arched a brow at him.

"Sure, we can do that. This is one of the attractions. We've got a beautiful town square, don't you think?" He sat down on the bench, and she sat down beside him.

"Oh, absolutely. This landscaping is wonderful. And that old bronze statue over there is so picturesque." She took a bite of her doughnut, delighted by how delicious it was.

"That's the town founder. And the landscaping was designed in the nineteen twenties."

"Wow, you really are a tour guide, aren't you?"

He laughed, taking another bite of his doughnut. For a few moments, they were both quiet, looking out at the beautiful town square and enjoying the wonderful taste of their pastries and drinks.

"What's first on our agenda, Fearless Leader?" Noelle's tone was playful, and she found herself squirming with curiosity. She didn't know what kind of place he was going to take her to see first.

"First, we're going to go hiking on the prettiest trail in the whole state."

"The prettiest, huh? In the whole state? That's high praise."

"Oh, it's well deserved. Especially now that the leaves are starting to change color. And when you get higher up, there are stone bluffs, and sometimes you're in the woods, and sometimes you've got this breathtaking view of the ocean—just wait. You'll see that I'm right in just a little bit."

She laughed. "You're making a pretty convincing argument."

They finished their pastries and then set off walking together, sipping their beverages and keeping up a lighthearted conversation. Noelle felt the cool breeze brush against her cheeks, and every time she took a deep breath, she could smell the spicy aroma of autumn.

They made their way across town, toward the park that held the entrance to the hiking trail. As they went, Dean pointed out various charming old buildings, explaining when they were built and what they were currently being used for. He knew a surprising amount of Rosewood Beach history, and Noelle was impressed both by his knowledge and the easy, friendly manner in which he communicated the information.

Soon they reached the head of the trail. Noelle found herself grinning as she looked down the charming avenue of trees that opened up in front of her and Dean.

"This is lovely." She looked up at the branches rustling overhead. Some of the trees were still green, but others had gorgeous yellow, orange, or fiery red leaves. Sunlight gleamed on the leaves, and the brilliant blue of the sky was visible beyond the flickering colors.

"I told you," Dean said, chuckling. "I never lie."

She smiled, feeling grateful that things had worked out the way they had. She was glad that going exploring alone hadn't really worked out for her, and that her car troubles had led her to becoming closer to Dean.

Dean glanced at Noelle as she walked beside him and he smiled. He felt tired, but for the time being, his energy was able to keep up with the tour that he'd planned for her. She'd been loving every second of it, and he found her enthusiasm contagious. She seemed to pour new life into him in a way that helped him maintain his energy even after all of the walking they'd done.

After a breathtaking hike through the woods and along the coast, they'd stopped for a delicious lunch at Ocean Breeze Café. Dean had ordered a buffalo chicken cheesesteak sandwich with sides of coleslaw and homemade sea salt and vinegar potato chips, and Noelle had laughed as she'd ordered the same thing. She'd sworn she wasn't trying to copy him, and she had genuinely decided on the same meal before he'd ordered his.

They'd both enjoyed the food immensely, and after they were done eating, Dean had felt refreshed and energized. From there, their exploring took them to all of Rosewood Beach's attractions, including historical landmarks, cozy shops, and a little model train museum that Noelle had proclaimed to be absolutely enchanting.

"Where are you taking me now, Fearless

Leader?" Her eyes were bright with interest as she looked at him. "It's our final destination, right?"

He grinned. He loved that she kept calling him "Fearless Leader." It made him feel braver than he really was, since he'd definitely had his moments of struggling with fear and uncertainty since receiving his diagnosis. "You're right, it is our final destination, but it's a secret. You'll have to wait and see. Do you trust me?"

"What, after all that? Of course. At this point, if you told me to jump out of a moving car, I'd trust you."

He shook his head. "I would never ask you to jump out of a moving car."

"Well, see? That's more reason for me to trust you."

They laughed together, the sound of it echoing slightly off the sides of the buildings they were walking beside. They were in a quiet part of town, near the hardware store and the town hall. It was the part of town that was less spruced up for tourists and looked more genuinely lived-in. Noelle didn't seem any less impressed with it, however. Her eyes still held a sparkle of fascination as she gazed around her.

They turned a corner and found themselves in

front of another little park. This one offered a beautiful view of the ocean and had a charming little playground on one side of it. There were a few kids there, laughing and shrieking with mirth as they swung on the swing set and chased each other down the slide.

"Is this our final destination?" Noelle asked, turning to him with a warm smile. "I think that's so sweet."

He shook his head, smiling back at her. "It's almost our final destination. Follow me."

He led her across the park, near to the place where the grass gave way to a short stretch of sand leading to the ocean. There, a massive oak tree stood, offering a wide expanse of shade. Its sides were covered in carvings, making it look like some kind of magical thing.

"This," Dean said, as proudly as if he'd made it himself, "is the oldest tree in town."

"Wow." She gazed at it as if she was genuinely captivated by it, and he watched her for a few moments, feeling a surge of admiration for her kindhearted, warm spirit.

He felt a wave of fatigue come over him, and he let out a quiet sigh of relief, glad that this was the last stop on the tour he'd planned for her. He'd been enjoying every minute of their day together, but he had to admit that he was ready to sit down.

"Look at all of the different carvings," she said, touching one gently with her fingertips. "They add so much character to something that's so beautiful already."

He nodded. "All the couples in town carve their initials into the tree. That's why it's so covered. I mean, look, even up there." He pointed to where some people had carved their initials onto one of the branches. "It's been a town tradition since the nineteen-forties."

"Oh, I love that." She crouched down, getting a closer look at some of the lower carvings. "That's such a sweet tradition."

"Yeah, it really is." He found himself watching her, noticing the way the wind blew back wisps of her hair from her face.

*I'm surprised she hasn't been taken off the market yet*, he thought. *She's such a sweet, genuine person. She deserves the best man.*

"Well, I think this tree is one of my absolute favorite things on this whole tour, which is really saying a lot." She stood up with a smile. "But the whole tour has been amazing, thank you so much, Dean."

"Of course. Happy to show you around. Hopefully you feel like you have more of a solid footing around here now."

"Oh, I definitely do."

The two of them began to stroll toward a nearby picnic table, as if they'd reached an unspoken agreement that they'd like to sit there together for a while.

"I had no idea that such a small town could have so much to offer," she said, sitting down. "What was it like to grow up here? I bet it was great."

The leaves of the oak tree rustled overhead, adding a gentle music to the already soothing sound of the nearby surf. Dean found himself feeling content and happy in a way that he hadn't felt in a long time—possibly even more than he'd ever felt before.

"It was great." His mind traced over a multitude of memories, of bike rides with his friends, of night walks with his family, of ice cream socials and clam bakes and baseball games. "The people here are really good to be around. Everyone kind of bands together, you know? We're here for each other. It's great to live in a place like that."

She nodded. "I'm definitely getting that sense." The smile on her face when she looked at him was so warm and endearing that Dean found himself needing to look away for a moment.

"I've always loved it here," he said, watching the sunlight flicker on the ocean waves. "And I know my whole family feels the same way. Two of my sisters, Julia and Alexis, both moved away to big cities. Julia moved to New York and Alexis moved to L.A. They lived there for a while, but both of them ended up moving back to stay. And I think it's more than just the fact that our family is here, and we all want to be close together. I think it's also just the town itself, you know? People know how to live calm, steady lives here. They're not rushing around all stressed out all the time like how people are in the city."

Noelle nodded. "Sometimes cities are so loud it's like you can't think. And it's not just the literal noise I'm talking about either. There are so many opinions and passions and people telling you how you need to think and be. Rosewood Beach isn't like that. It's like people know how to slow down and really be themselves here."

"That's a frankly brilliant way of putting it," he said, grinning at her.

She waved a hand. "I don't know that it's brilliant, but... well, it's something I've observed.

Even before I moved here. Whenever I came to visit my grandparents, I got that sense."

"See, you too. People can't seem to stay away from Rosewood Beach. Everyone ends up coming back to stay."

She laughed. "What's the town's secret, do you think? Where's that irresistible magnetic pull coming from?"

"Oh, definitely The Lighthouse Grill's unbeatable corned beef and hash. Everyone who tries to leave gets sucked back in by it."

She laughed. "And the Seaside Sweets Bakery's Grasshopper. That was the best drink I've ever had."

"And those doughnuts."

"Oh, absolutely. And I had a root beer float at the pub once. It was so good, I could have sworn there was some kind of secret ingredient in it."

They kept going back and forth, listing foods they'd eaten in Rosewood Beach and loved, and before long, both of them were doubled over in a mutual laughing attack. It wasn't that what they'd been saying was particularly funny, Dean thought, it was that they both seemed to be in a giddy mood. He was enjoying bantering with her so much that he felt especially inclined to laugh.

"Oh, wow," Noelle said, wiping away a tear. "I

guess we solved the mystery. The best thing about Rosewood Beach is its food."

They smiled at each other, both of them knowing that wasn't really the answer. The best thing about Rosewood Beach was its company, and he felt another rush of gratitude that he'd gotten to spend such a long, fun day with her.

"Well," she said regretfully as she stood up, "I think it's time for me to head on home. Today was amazing, but as your physical therapist, I suggest you use the evening to rest."

He nodded, putting on an exaggeratedly serious expression. "I wouldn't dare argue with the best PT around."

She laughed. "The best, huh? Well, you were the best tour guide, Fearless Leader."

They walked back to the town square, where they'd parked their cars. They said breezy, almost affectionate goodbyes and parted ways. Dean glanced over his shoulder at her a couple of times as he walked back to his car.

His stomach growled, telling him that it was time for dinner. Once he'd gotten inside his car, however, instead of starting to drive toward home, he found himself just sitting there with a goofy grin on his face.

*She is the best,* he thought. Not just the best PT. *Right now, I'm pretty sure she's just kind of the best in general.*

His stomach growled again, and he started his car and started to make his way back home. He did feel fatigued and ready for some quality rest. He also felt emotionally and mentally energized, however. It had been a wonderful day, and he was looking forward to the next time he would see Noelle.

# CHAPTER NINETEEN

Alexis bustled around in front of her stove, finishing preparing the food that she was getting ready for herself and Dean. She'd invited her brother over for lunch, and she was looking forward to hearing his updates on how physical therapy was going.

She leaned over the skillet, in which she was frying chicken, onions, and slices of red bell peppers. She was making chicken fajitas, since she knew that it was one of Dean's favorite meals and one that she and Grayson enjoyed as well. She thought to herself with a pleased smile that the kitchen smelled absolutely incredible.

She placed the lid back on the skillet and turned the heat to low. She went over to the cupboard and got out a set of clean dishes. She set them on the table along with a pitcher of sparkling iced tea that she'd made earlier that day. She took a step back from the table and admired the look of it. She had mint green placemats on it, which paired beautifully with the light birch wood of the table. In the center of the table was a little ceramic pumpkin that Grayson had given her, and she thought it added a cozy vibe to the setting.

She finished preparing the meal just before she heard the doorbell ring. Grinning eagerly, she hurried down the hallway and opened the front door.

Dean was standing there, a big smile on his face. "For you," he said, handing her a package of store-bought mint chocolate cookies. "As a thank you for feeding me."

"Aww, you didn't need to do that! I was feeding you as a thank-you for fixing our internet issues."

"No, you're feeding me as an excuse to interrogate me about my life. You want to know all about physical therapy and if I've met any women I want to marry yet." Dean was laughing, but she thought she saw the tips of his ears turn slightly pink as he spoke.

She shook her head, chuckling. "You know me too well. At least you came over anyway."

"Well, I can't resist chicken fajitas, you know that. And you're okay too."

He dodged her hand as she tried to swat him and hurried ahead of her into the kitchen.

"Wow, it smells amazing in here," he said, grinning as he stood in the middle of the room and inhaled the smell of the food.

"Why thank you." She caught up to him and gave him the swat that he'd dodged. He pretended to double over in pain and she laughed. "Grayson might join us in a little bit, he's locked up in his office working on something."

"Uh oh." Dean looked concerned. "Is he falling back into his workaholic habits?"

She shook her head, smiling. "No, he isn't. It's—well, he's working on something for me." Before Dean could ask her what that was, she took him by the shoulders and sat him down in one of the kitchen chairs. "Eat your food while it's hot. You know you're here so I can find out all about your life. Tell me how everything's going."

"That," he said cheerfully as he started to dish food onto his plate, "sounds like an excuse to talk with my mouth full."

She shook her head, laughing. "I'm being serious. You seem as though you have more energy than usual. Is that true? Is physical therapy going well?"

He nodded, and there was a light of joy in his eyes that make her heart beat faster with happiness for him. "Yeah, physical therapy is going really well. I have so much more energy than usual. I mean, yesterday I walked around a lot, and I got tired, but it really wasn't too bad. I mean, that much hiking around would have tired me out in the past too. Maybe not as much, but it's clear that my stamina is improving."

"Dean, that's fantastic! I'm so happy to hear that." She was about to ask him more about why he went for such a long walk the day before, but at that moment Grayson stepped into the room.

"Hey, sweetheart." Grayson hurried over to her and gave her a kiss on the lips. "Hey, Dean." He smiled at Dean for a moment, but then he held out a notebook, showing Alexis what was written on the first page of it. "I've been analyzing numbers and I've come up with the prices for your jewelry. Based on market value and quality and the fact that your business is currently an unknown. I've also worked out what would be the most cost-effective way to order materials, and I've created a flow chart for increasing sales. The first thing you should do is create a website. I can help you with that."

Alexis felt a rush of joy over everything Grayson was telling her, but she didn't want to be rude by having a private conversation in front of Dean. "Thank you, sweetheart, that's amazing. Can we talk about it more later, though?"

"Sure." Grayson glanced at Dean with a grin. "Enjoy your lunch, Dean."

"Thanks." Dean smiled at him, although his eyebrows were lifted curiously. He was clearly wondering what Grayson was talking about. "Are you going to eat with us?"

"No, sorry." Grayson shook his head. "I'm expecting a phone call from my mother in a few minutes, and I have to admit, I've really got the itch to keep working on all these figures. I want to work on other aspects of the business too, Alexis, like advertising and finding craft fairs—well, I'll tell you later. You'll see in no time that launching this venture is more than reasonable." Grinning and clearly enthused, Grayson left the kitchen.

Alexis realized that her heart was beating faster with excitement. Everything that Grayson was talking about seemed too good to be true. She could hardly believe that she was about to start trying to sell her jewelry as part of a legitimate business. She felt nervous and uncertain, but also eager in a way that filled her with adrenaline. She was thankful that she had Grayson by her side to lead her through the tricky process of starting a business.

"What was that all about?" Dean asked curiously as soon as Grayson had walked out of the room.

"Well, the other day I was making jewelry during my lunch break at the pub." She smiled as she remembered it. "I've just started picking up the hobby again. You remember I used to make jewelry sometimes?"

"Oh, yeah. I remember that pair of earrings you made for Grandma. They were really beautiful— they had those kind of sparkly, bigger purple beads and then the little strands of colored beads woven into a pattern."

"Wow." Alexis smiled at him, touched that he'd remembered the earrings in so much detail. "I remember those too—they were really fun to make."

"And you're really good at making jewelry. It's one thing to just enjoy a hobby, and another to actually be very skilled at it. I think painting is fun, but I'm no good at it. You're actually really good at making jewelry."

"Thanks." She smiled at him, feeling grateful for his support. "That means a lot to me, and I value your opinion."

"As you should." Her brother nodded sagely.

Alexis laughed. "So anyway, Grayson saw me making jewelry at the pub that day, and I guess he thinks that I can sell my creations for money. It seems like a wild idea to me, but Grayson's obviously an experienced businessman, so it would be silly for me not to trust him. He's been working out all the details. That's what that was there."

"All the dots are connecting." Dean grinned. "Alexis, I love that! I think you're going to have a lot of fun and start making a living doing what you love."

"Well, the fun part is for sure." She laughed. "We'll see if any money ever comes of it."

"You've got a good partner in there." Dean jerked his thumb toward Grayson's home office. "He clearly believes in you, and so do I."

"Thank you." She beamed at him. "I think it's sweet that when Grayson saw me doing something that I love, it gave him so many ideas, you know? I love it when we can be creative for each other. Not just me and Grayson, but all of us. It's one of the most beautiful things about love, I think."

"Huh. That's a nice thought." Dean was quiet for a few moments, and Alexis became curious.

"Penny for your thoughts," she said and took a bite of her spicy chicken fajita.

"Oh, well, I was thinking about a friend of mine. I mean, I'm sure what you just said applies to friendships too."

"Yeah?" Alexis's eyebrows lifted, and she realized she was talking with her mouth full. "What friendship?" Dean looked slightly bashful in a way that aroused her suspicions.

"Well, actually I've become pretty good friends with my physical therapist, Noelle," he said, taking a hurried sip of his iced tea. "She got her car fixed at my shop, you know, and we've struck up a kind of friendship. She's always a great person to be around, but seeing her in her element is really something. I mean, when she's leading our PT sessions." He looked thoughtful for a moment, and Alexis found herself practically squirming.

"So, you like her?" she asked after a few seconds.

"As a person? Yeah, she's great. I liked her right away from our first appointment, but now I like her more than ever. With each session I'm realizing more and more how good she is at her job. It gives me a perspective of her that I wouldn't have had if I'd just met her on the street. I mean, she's sweet and good natured, but I really respect her now because I've seen her in her element so much."

Alexis immediately perked up when she heard her brother talking about Noelle so favorably. "Uh huh." Her mind was racing a mile a minute. She watched Dean's face carefully, and she thought she saw the tips of his ears turning pinkish again.

*Dean never talks about women*, she thought. *Could it just be that she's his physical therapist and they've become friends, or is he interested in her in a special way?*

"What kinds of things does she do that make you feel she's good at her job?" she asked, nonchalantly taking a sip of her iced tea.

"She's very encouraging, but also pushes me to work hard. She's good at knowing when I need to quit and when I need to persevere. It's almost like she's got a sixth sense or something. This food is really good, by the way, thank you."

Alexis shook her head. "No changing the subject, please. Does she think your symptoms are going to keep improving?"

"She's never said that for sure, but I think that's just because she doesn't want to get my hopes up too much. She always speaks in terms of potential outcomes, but I mean, my symptoms are improving. She definitely knows how to get me to feel better."

"That's wonderful." Alexis's heart stirred with happiness for her brother. "I'm so happy to hear that."

"Thanks." He smiled and let out a cheerful sigh of relief. "It does feel really good knowing that there's something that's going to help."

"And Noelle sounds like the perfect woman for the job," Alexis said. "What else do you like about her? You said she was encouraging."

Dean shrugged, and Alexis noticed that the tips of his ears were definitely pink then. "She's just a really kind, genuine person. I like spending time with her."

"Just in your sessions? Or have you two hung out outside of PT?"

Dean cleared his throat gently. "I did end up showing her around town yesterday. She'd been wanting to go on a tour of Rosewood Beach when her car had broken down. I told her I'd give her a tour. Seemed like the neighborly thing to do."

"Oh, definitely," Alexis said, and she was grinning so hard that Dean gave her a look. "That was really nice of you." She waited a few heartbeats, watching the way he was blushing, before saying,

"Do you think that there might be a spark between you two? I mean, a romantic one?"

Dean shook his head, laughing. "Oh, please stop with the matchmaking, Alexis. Just because she's a girl and we get along, it doesn't mean we're going to start dating. Like I said, I was just trying to be nice. She's a friend of mine, and she's new in town. We're just friends."

"Okay." Alexis sighed, feeling disappointed but believing her brother's words. Secretly, she was hoping that his friendship with Noelle would turn out to be more than just a friendship. She immediately got a swarm of ideas for how she could try to nudge Noelle and Dean toward starting to fall for each other romantically.

*I guess what we were saying earlier is true,* she thought to herself with a chuckle. *You do get creative ideas when you want to help out someone you love. Just like Grayson wants to help me with my jewelry business because he sees I'm in my element there, I want to help Dean find love with this Noelle girl. He seems like he's in his element when he talks about her —it's clear she makes him happy and comfortable.*

"Well, thanks for telling me about her." She smiled as she lifted her fajita off her plate again. "I'd love to meet her sometime."

"Yeah, you probably will. It's a small town," Dean answered vaguely, winking.

Their conversation turned toward other things as they continued to eat, but Alexis's mind kept wandering back to the subject of her brother and Noelle. She wanted to meet Noelle and get a better sense of whether she and her brother were really compatible or not. She had a feeling that they were, and she knew that she was going to be in a state of happy suspense until she found out more from Dean about how his "friendship" with Noelle was progressing.

*　*　*

Dean stepped out of his car, grinning in eagerness. He was at Shawn's used car lot, and he couldn't help feeling excited when he was near so many wonderful old cars. Most of them had already been refurbished and were ready to sell, but toward the back of the lot were the cars that needed a lot of work before they could be sold. He knew that was where Shawn was going to meet him to show him the Ford Mustang.

As he walked across the parking lot, admiring the cars he saw, he thought about his lunch with Alexis earlier that day. He'd enjoyed spending time with his sister and the fajitas had been especially delicious, but the way Alexis had implied that he and Noelle had a romantic spark beginning between them had made him feel restless. He wasn't ready to admit to himself that he liked the idea of that being true. Noelle was friendly and kind, but he had no reason to believe that she saw him as anything more than a friend, and he didn't want to get his hopes up.

*I'll just focus on cars today,* he thought with a chuckle. *Cars I know how to handle. Romance, not so much.*

A moment later, he saw Shawn waiting for him at the back of the parking lot. Shawn was a big guy with a bushy red beard, and he had a personality as thunderous as his voice.

"Dean!" Shawn gave him a big bear hug. "It's so good to see you."

"So good to see you too, Shawn." Dean grinned at his friend, feeling glad to see him. "It's been too long."

"You're so right. We won't let time get away from us again like this."

They stood there for a while catching up and bantering. Then Shawn jerked his thumb over his shoulder, pointing toward the Ford Mustang that was parked behind him.

"You want to take a look at her? She's yours if you want. Needs a lot of work, but I don't need to tell you how satisfying it would be to get her up and running again."

"No, you don't." Dean gazed in admiration at the car. "Wow, it really is beautiful."

"Told you." Shawn grinned as Dean began to check out the car, looking under the hood and inspecting the doors and windows. "The body is in great condition, it's just that engine. And a couple of the headlights, but those are an easy fix."

"Not when the parts I need were made decades ago," Dean said, laughing, but he felt excited. It was more fun to try to put together a challenge than something that was just going to put itself back together.

"What do you think?" Shawn asked. "You want it?"

"I mean, yeah." Dean laughed, feeling a kind of thrill go through him. "That would be amazing—"

As he spoke, he noticed another car over Shawn's shoulder. It was a Porsche, and it appeared to be on the older side.

"What about that one over there?" Dean asked, nodding his head toward the vehicle. "What year is it?"

"That Porsche? Ah, another beauty I don't have time to fix up. That one is a 1988."

Dean's eyebrows lifted. It was the same year as the Porsche that Noelle had fixed up with her grandfather—the car she'd wanted to get to ride in but hadn't gotten a chance to. All at once, he became enchanted with the idea of fixing it up.

"How much to take that one off your hands?" he asked.

"What, both of them?" Shawn grinned. "And earlier you weren't sure you even wanted the one."

Dean shrugged, smiling. "Well, I'd actually like to start with that Porsche. But like you said, if I end up not having the energy, I can take things slow."

Shawn nodded. "Well, sounds like a good deal for both of us. She doesn't run, that Porsche, but she's in better condition than this one here. I'll charge you a little less than what I would a stranger, though."

"No, you don't need to do that." Dean shook his head. "I can afford it."

They talked prices for a little while, and the price that Shawn suggested for the Porsche Dean felt was more than fair, and it was well within his budget. He bought it on the spot, deciding then and there that it was going to be the car he worked on first.

He and Shawn worked out a delivery plan for the cars, and then he got back into his own car and began to drive away. As he made his way along the picturesque roads, back to Rosewood Beach, he felt an excitement pulsing through him that put a huge smile on his face.

# CHAPTER TWENTY

"And then, the airplane went zoom! Right into Macey's mouth!"

Julia chuckled as she watched Cooper spoon-feeding his little daughter at the dinner table. Macey was more than capable of using her own spoon and toddler fork, but she didn't like to eat her vegetables, so Cooper was resorting to the airplane method. It was working beautifully, and Cooper's antics and Macey's adorable giggles were providing excellent dinner entertainment for Julia.

The three of them were sharing a delicious meal of breaded cod, mashed potatoes, and steamed broccoli. Julia had come over to Cooper's house earlier in the evening and helped him prepare the meal, which had been a nice, quiet time the two of them shared while Macey was playing with her toys.

"Someday, you're going to love broccoli, Macey," Julia told the toddler, leaning forward conspiratorially. "I used to hate broccoli, and now—" She took a dramatic bite of her broccoli and sighed happily—"I love it."

Cooper laughed more at Julia's performance than Macey did, but Julia was delighted by the way Macey nodded tentatively a moment later.

"Okay," the little girl said, clearly doubting that she could ever love something so horrible as broccoli.

"My mom used to cover our broccoli in cheese," Julia said to Cooper. "I mean, not cover. But she put a fair amount of cheese on it, and that's really delicious. Even for kids. It might be a good way of getting Macey to want to eat her broccoli."

Cooper frowned for a few seconds, and Julia's heart sank.

*He's going to tell me he doesn't like that idea,* she thought with a stomach-flop of disappointment. *It seems that whatever I suggest when it comes to raising Macey, he likes his way of doing things better.*

To her surprise, however, Cooper nodded. "That's a great idea, thanks. Macey does really love cheese."

"Yeah? Great!" Julia found herself grinning. She made a tiny fist bump for herself out of sight, underneath the table. For the first time, Cooper had accepted her parenting advice. It made her feel relieved and hopeful that he was going to allow her to care for Macey more in the future.

"But then again," Cooper said, frowning again, "cheese isn't as healthy as vegetables, and I hate for her to learn at an early age that it's okay to eat less healthy things just because they taste better. I'll have to think about it."

Julia repressed a groan and did her best to smile at Cooper.

*I can't win,* she thought, wanting to sigh but restraining herself. *Gosh, that's disappointing.*

Still, she told herself, she wasn't going to let it ruin her evening. She was still having a wonderful time with Cooper and Macey, and the food was delicious. Cooper started telling her a story about the insane amount of gnomes that one of his landscaping clients had, and before long she was almost doubled over with laughter. Macey was giggling too, seeming to be delighted by how much the adults were amused.

"What do you think, Macey?" Julia asked, wiping away a tear. "Do you like gnomes?"

"No." Macey shook her head. "No beards."

"She doesn't like beards," Cooper said, chuckling. "So gnomes are out. At least for now. Her dislike of beards has only lasted for a week, we'll see how long it goes."

"Better not take her over to that house," Julia teased. "That's too many beards."

Cooper belted out a laugh, but in the next moment, he pulled his phone out of his pocket with a frown.

"Work is calling," he said. "That's weird that they're calling so late. I'm sorry, sweetheart." He leaned over and gave Julia a quick kiss before answering the phone. "Hello?"

Julia watched as Cooper's eyebrows lifted and his lips parted in surprise.

"Oh, no," he said. "Yes, yes, I can. I'll be there in twenty minutes."

"What happened?" Julia asked, feeling worried, as soon as he'd hung up.

"There's an electrical issue at the Greener Pastures offices," he said. "I guess I'm the only one who has experience as an electrician, and they want me to come in and make sure nothing's a fire hazard before the electric company can get there."

"Oh, gosh." Julia shuddered. "Be careful."

"I will." He smiled at her. "I'm sure it's all fine, but I agree with them that we should be cautious. I need to go in and look things over, but I'll be back soon. I'm really sorry."

"It's not a problem at all," she assured him, squeezing his hand. "Life happens."

"I know, but—well, would you be able to tuck Macey in tonight? I don't think I'll get back before her bedtime."

Julia's heart leapt up. He was trusting her to take care of Macey by herself! She nodded, smiling reassuringly at him. "No worries. I'd be happy to."

Cooper was already standing up and walking to the back door, where his shoes were. "If you have any questions, you can—no, I guess you'd better not call me for a while."

"It'll be fine." Julia smiled at him. "Please be safe, and we'll see you soon."

"Okay." Cooper finished hurriedly tying his shoes. "See you later, my girls." He gave Julia and Macey quick forehead kisses and then slipped out the back door.

Macey watched him go dubiously, her bottom lip quivering.

"Don't worry, Macey," Julia assured the little girl

warmly. "He's coming right back. Should we finish our dinner?"

Now that she was alone with the toddler, she did feel suddenly nervous. What if Macey had a meltdown and she didn't know how to get her to stop crying?

But after a few seconds, Macey smiled and nodded. Thankfully, she'd already eaten all of her broccoli, and she liked the rest of her food and didn't hesitate to eat it.

When their meal was over, Julia left the dirty dishes on the table, deciding to clean up the kitchen after she'd gotten Macey to go to sleep.

"Time for bed, Macey," she said, scooping the toddler up into her arms. "You're so sleepy, aren't you? Wow."

Macey shook her head, but in the next moment she let out a big yawn and Julia laughed. She carried Macey upstairs to her bedroom, starting to wonder what it was she needed to do first.

*What is her normal bedtime routine?* she thought, biting her lip. *I don't want to get it wrong. I should have asked Cooper before he left!*

She pondered it, and as she was thinking, Macey pressed her cheek against Julia's. The toddler's face was so sticky that Julia knew her next move in an instant. Macey would need to take a bath before going to bed.

"Okay, Macey, time for a bath," Julia said. "So you can get all nice and clean."

"Yay!"

Julia laughed, glad that the toddler wasn't going to fight her about it. She made a nice bubble bath for Macey, making sure the water wasn't too hot or too cold. She let Macey play with her bath toys for a little while before drying her off and helping her get into her pajamas.

By that point, Macey was starting to look genuinely sleepy, but Julia knew she needed to stay awake a little bit longer so that she could brush her teeth.

"Are you ready for the toothbrush song?" she asked Macey as she picked up her toothbrush and added a dollop of toothpaste to the bristles.

Macey looked confused, and Julia laughed. "You need to let me brush your teeth while I sing the toothbrush song, okay? Ready?"

Macey nodded and Julia began to sing silly lyrics about being a toothbrush and missing Macey's teeth. Macey began to laugh as Julia brushed her teeth, but the song seemed to do the trick. By the time they were walking back to Macey's bedroom together, hand-in-hand, both of them were still laughing a little.

"You want to hear a story before bed, Macey?" Julia asked.

"Yeah!" Macey scampered over to her little bookshelf and pulled out a couple of her favorite picture books.

Julia sat down in the rocker placed by Macey's window and the toddler climbed into her lap. They cuddled together while Julia read a picture book about bugs starting a bakery. By the time she was finished with it, Macey was sound asleep.

Julia sat there quietly for a few moments, treasuring her time with the little girl.

*I've been wanting this for weeks,* she thought. *Time for me to bond with Macey, and a chance to see if I really could be a good parent to her. I think the answer is definitely yes.*

At that moment, she heard the sound of the back door opening and closing downstairs. She listened to the sound of Cooper's footsteps as he made his way up the staircase. A moment later he appeared in the doorway of Macey's room, and his face lit up into a big smile when he saw the two of them together.

"Hey there," he whispered. He tiptoed forward

and gave Julia a kiss. "Look at you two. Did everything go well tonight?"

"Very well," she whispered back. "She took a bubble bath and I brushed her teeth. We read one book and then she fell sound asleep."

Cooper gazed down at the two of them with a sweet smile on his face, clearly touched. "That's great. That makes me really happy."

"Me too," she whispered. She wrapped Macey in her arms and stood up carefully. She carried the little girl over to her crib and set her down in it. She tucked the covers up around her chin and bent over to kiss her forehead.

When she turned around, she saw that Cooper was watching her with tears sparkling in his eyes. He took her into his arms and gave her a bear hug.

"Should we go downstairs?" he whispered.

She nodded, and they went back downstairs together, hand-in-hand. Once they were downstairs in the living room, he kissed her.

"Thank you for taking such good care of my daughter," he said. "It means a lot to me."

Julia felt tears rush into her eyes. His approval was such a relief to her, since she'd wanted him to see her as capable of taking care of Macey for so long.

"What's wrong?" he asked, seeing her tears and holding her tightly. "Is everything okay?"

"Yes," she said, laughing through her tears. "It's just that—well, I was worried that you would never trust me as a caregiver to Macey if we ever get married. I kept trying to do things for her, and it seemed like everything I did or suggested wasn't okay with you. I was starting to feel like I never did anything right when it came to taking care of her. I really wanted you to trust me, but you kept wanting to do everything differently from how I was trying to do it."

"Oh, sweetheart." Cooper gave her a tight hug. "I'm so sorry I made you feel that way. I absolutely didn't mean to. I understand what you're saying—I did keep on doing things my own way even when you tried to help. But I didn't mean that as any kind of a criticism to you. I'm just so used to doing things my own way."

"I understand that." She wiped away her last remaining tears, smiling warmly at him.

"I wish you'd told me you felt that way," he said. "There's room for me to change the way I parent Macey. You're a kind, intelligent person and I think you have wonderful ideas. I would have been more willing to consider them if I'd known you were feeling this way."

Julia nodded. "Mom said that I should talk to you about it, but I don't know. I guess I didn't feel ready. It feels kind of strange to be bringing up the possibility of us being married when we aren't engaged."

"Oh, it's not so strange." His eyes warmed as he brushed his thumbs over her cheeks. "I think it's smart to look ahead like that. And I want you to know that I do trust you. I hope one day we'll be parenting together. As a team."

Julia gazed at him, her heart leaping up in joy. "That thought makes me really happy," she whispered.

"Me too," he said, and the two of them shared a kiss.

# CHAPTER TWENTY-ONE

Noelle took a long, leisurely sip of her coffee as she looked over her PT schedule. She was sitting at her desk, blinking complacently, until she noticed an appointment on her schedule for the day that hadn't been there earlier in the week.

"Dean!" she mouthed, feeling suddenly excited.

She told herself that her excitement was due to the fact that she was glad that he was taking his physical therapy work so seriously. He'd been scheduling extra appointments lately, and she was always glad to work with him. She thought the world of him and she wanted to see him improving in his symptoms.

She did busy work in her office for a little while longer, and then it was time for Dean's appointment.

She sat at her desk, glancing expectantly at her door every few moments as she tried to work on going through her emails.

Then all at once there was a soft knock on her office door.

"Come on in!"

Dean pushed open the door to her office, smiling. Noelle grinned when she saw him, and then she noticed that he had something in his hands. It was a beautiful bouquet of pink carnations.

"Hey, Dean! Good to see you."

"Hey." He walked up to her desk and handed her the bouquet. "These are for you."

"I—why—they're beautiful," she stammered, feeling as though she might be blushing. "How did you know I love carnations?"

"Well, when we were in the general store during our Rosewood Beach tour, you were admiring the bouquets of carnations. And as far as pink goes, that was a lucky guess." He chuckled.

She took a deep breath of the bouquet, enjoying the way the smooth, delicate flower petals felt against her nose. The bouquet made her happy in a way she wasn't used to feeling—she felt almost lightheaded, and although she felt special, she also suddenly felt self-conscious.

"These are very beautiful. I hardly know what to say. What's the occasion?"

"Just a thank you for being such a great physical therapist. I really feel as though my symptoms are improving, and I'm grateful."

"I'm so happy to hear that."

For a moment, they stood there smiling at each other, neither of them seeming to know what to say.

"Thank you. I know just where I want to put these in my apartment. There's a spot on my kitchen counter that catches the light beautifully. I've got a blue glass vase I can put these in."

"Sounds lovely."

"And thank you again for showing me around town. I feel like I know Rosewood Beach so much better than I did before."

"I had a great time, truly. It was a really fun day."

"I'm glad. Speaking of which..." Her posture straightened and her manner became more brisk as she switched over into work mode. "That brings me to the first item on our agenda for today. I want to ask you about how your symptoms have been improving and about your progress with at-home exercises. How was your fatigue after our very long hike around town?"

"Not too bad. I slept soundly that night, let me

tell you." He laughed. "But overall, I didn't feel particularly tired the next day. I felt a little more achy than usual, but it was like I was tired and had more energy at the same time."

She nodded. "Yes! The difference between just feeling tired and fatigue caused by factors other than physical exertion. I'm so glad to hear that. How have your at-home exercises been going?"

"Good. Really good. I've missed them here and there, but for the most part I'm making sure to get them done. They really seem to be helping."

"Amazing." Noelle smiled as she jotted down notes. "Tell me more about that."

As Dean told her more details about his exercising and the symptom relief that was resulting from it, it became clear to her that he had made significant progress since his first session.

"That's wonderful," she said, clasping her hands enthusiastically. "Look at this chart here. Based on what you've told me, your symptom improvement is correlated to your participating in the exercises in this way. Does that look right to you?"

She turned the screen of her computer toward him, showing him the chart she'd made. It showed in clear details the improvement that Dean's symptoms had made.

"Yes." He grinned, his eyes lighting up. "That does look right. It's really exciting to see it in a clear picture like that."

"It really is exciting."

For a moment, their eyes met, and she could feel the shared excitement arcing between them like an electric current. In that moment, Noelle realized that she shared a connection with him like she'd never shared with anyone before. And she knew that she was attracted to him. Her heart began to beat wildly in her chest and her smile faded, but she couldn't look away.

Dean held her gaze as well, also looking suddenly starstruck. For a few wild moments, she felt as though she couldn't breathe, and then she forced herself to snap out of it.

*This is a professional setting,* Noelle, she reminded herself. *You need to keep romance out of your office.*

"But of course it's important that you keep up the good work," she said, tearing her eyes away from Dean and smiling briskly. She took a deep breath, willing her heart rate to go down. "You seem to be well on your way to making these at-home exercises a regular habit. That's the best thing you can do for yourself—put in the work, and put it in enough that it becomes part of your regular routine. Then you're less likely to miss the exercises."

Out of the corner of her eye, she could see Dean nod. "Makes sense." He seemed to still be smiling, but she didn't look directly at him. She suddenly felt extremely shy.

"Do you usually do your exercises at a specific time of day? Or rather, at a specific point in your regular routine, such as before you brush your teeth before bed? That's the best way to solidify a habit."

"No, I haven't been. That's a good idea."

She turned her gaze back to him with a smile, and was relieved to find that she could look at him without feeling as though she was turning three different shades of red. He made her feel comfortable in a way that quickly put her at ease, despite her jitters from realizing that she was attracted to him.

They continued with his physical therapy appointment, neither of them making any kind of a comment on the moment that they'd shared.

Hazel watched her family members walking ahead of her on the sidewalk and her heart stirred with happiness. It was a brisk, sunny autumn day with a pale blue sky. She felt alert and alive and full of energy, and happy to be spending time with all of the women in the Owens family—but at the same time, her heart kept twisting with twinges of worry.

Hazel, Vivian, Julia, Alexis, and Samantha were out shopping for a dress for Samantha to wear to the dance. Samantha seemed absolutely giddy with excitement, and her aunts and grandmother were being supportive and cheerful, making sure the pre-teen felt special as they wandered from store to store.

Hazel wished that she was as carefree as everyone else seemed to be feeling. She was enjoying herself, that was without question, but she kept thinking about the boy that Samantha had confessed to having a crush on. She worried that Samantha would get hurt if he didn't ask her to the dance, and she worried that if he did ask her, he would end up treating her badly and she would get hurt anyway.

"Let's go in here!" Alexis said eagerly, stopping in front of a little antique store. "They have all kinds of vintage dresses in here. I remember some of them being really beautiful. And I bet a lot of them will have the kind of full skirts that you're looking for."

"Sounds great to me!" Samantha grinned eagerly. "I love old stuff."

They pushed open the door of the little shop, which jangled pleasantly. The antique store was clean and cozy and offered a beautiful display of whimsical and charming old objects.

"The clothing section is in the back of the store," Alexis said, leading them toward a doorway at the back of the room. "Follow me."

"I just know this is going to make me feel old," Vivian said, laughing. "I'm sure they'll have the kind of stuff I wore as a teenager on these racks. I guess that makes me an antique."

"Never," Julia said, laughing and kissing her mother's cheek. "Things only become antiques when they stop being the current fashion. You're always in fashion."

Vivian chuckled, looking happy. "Oh, tut."

"Gosh, this place is amazing!" Samantha scampered ahead, gazing up in delight at the two tiers of clothing racks. "I bet most of it won't fit me, but there's so much pretty stuff here."

"It might." Alexis grinned at her. "You're pretty tall for your age, and they made plenty of petite dresses back in the day. Let's see what we can find."

For a while, they all split up, going through the dresses one by one and cooing in delight over all the beautiful ones they found. Most of them looked too big for Samantha, but then Julia found a beautiful yellow satin dress that looked as though it might have been from the nineteen sixties.

"It doesn't quite fit with your Glinda theme, but it's so cute," Julia said, holding up the dress eagerly. "You want to try this one on?"

"I'd love to." Samantha looked at the dress as though it was made out of pure gold. Hazel felt an ache of nostalgic happiness in her heart, knowing that Samantha was about to experience so many of the joys of growing up.

They found the small changing room and Samantha went inside to put the dress on.

"Be sure to come out and show us," Vivian urged. "Even if you don't choose this one, I want a picture of you in it."

"I do too," Hazel said.

A moment later, Samantha stepped out of the changing room, wearing the yellow satin dress and practically glowing. She gave a twirl as her mom, grandmother, and aunts applauded.

"Here," Alexis said, handing her a pale blue dress with a tulle skirt. "Try this one on."

Samantha continued to try on dresses, even a few that were definitely not her size, just for fun. Hazel couldn't stop thinking about her daughter wearing one of the beautiful dresses to the dance, accompanied by the boy she had a crush on. Samantha looked so beautiful. She was sure to have many young men interested in her as she grew up, and Hazel didn't know how she was ever going to trust any boy or young man with her sweet girl.

Finally, she felt so overwhelmed she knew she was beginning to look as concerned as she felt. She didn't want to ruin everyone else's happy time together, and she decided to make an excuse so that she could slip away to have a moment to herself.

"I'm going to see if they have any cute shoes here," she said. "We'll need some good, comfortable shoes to go with the dress."

It was a flimsy excuse, since an antique store was not a good place to find shoes unless one was looking for some kind of novelty high heel, but she slipped quickly away before anyone could question her statement.

She turned a corner, looking for the shoes display she'd seen earlier. She took a deep breath, hoping her nerves would steady themselves. She felt jittery and almost close to tears. She loved seeing Samantha grow up, but it was also difficult for her because it made her think of all the different ways her daughter might get hurt.

She faced the charming rack of antique shoes, looking at it without really noticing what was in front of her. Her mind was spinning and she didn't know what to tell herself. She knew that pain was a natural part of life and that she couldn't protect Samantha from everything, but she still felt as though she wanted to make sure that nothing bad ever happened to her daughter.

"These are cute."

Hazel almost jumped as she realized that Julia had stepped up beside her. She turned to her sister with surprise, and saw that Julia was smiling at her sympathetically.

"Everything all right?" Julia asked gently. "You seem a little upset."

"I—I'm okay."

Julia shook her head. "Come on, Hazel, you can tell me. You were frowning back there whenever Samantha was in the changing room, and you looked like your smiles were kind of forced whenever she came out. And now you're off by yourself. Is something bothering you?"

Hazel sighed, grateful that her sister was so insightful. "You're right. Something is bothering me. I keep telling myself to let it go and just not think about it, but it seems I'm not really capable of doing that."

"What is it?" Julia asked gently, placing a sympathetic hand on Hazel's arm.

"It's this dance, I guess." Hazel took a deep breath and let out a long exhale. "She said that she's hoping—well, she wants this boy to go with her. And as far as I know, he hasn't asked her yet, and I'm worried she's going to get her hopes up and get hurt. Or what if he does ask her to the dance, but then he does something that hurts her later? I guess —it's just hard for me to see her growing up like this. I didn't realize we'd reached this stage yet, you know? The liking boys stage. I thought I had a little while longer before I would have to guide her through this."

Julia nodded. "But you're going to be so great at guiding her through this, I know you are."

Hazel found herself tearing up a little when she heard her sister's confident words. "Thank you for saying that. I know I'm going to do my best, but there are so many things to think about—I guess it all kind of came crashing down on me at once. I think I've been avoiding thinking about it. I've been wanting her to stay my little girl forever."

"Oh, I think she'll always be your little girl." Julia smiled as she wrapped an arm around Hazel. "I think we're all still Mom's little girls, and we will be no matter how old we get. But I know what you mean."

Hazel nodded, feeling comforted by Julia's encouragement. "Thank you." She laughed breathlessly. "How did you get to be so wise?"

"Oh, I wouldn't say I'm wise." Julia shook her head. "I've just been thinking about parenting a lot lately."

"Yeah? How come?"

"Well, I've been wanting to take more care of Macey—you know, take care of her on my own sometimes or do things like make her special snacks. Cooper is always grateful when I offer, but he's been having a hard time letting go of how he's always raised Macey and accepting my help. We finally had a good conversation about it, and I think he's reached a place where he's going to trust me more."

"That's great." Hazel smiled at her sister, glad she was sharing her heart with her. It made her feel less alone in her parenting struggles. "I'm sure he's going to continue to trust you more and more. You're a responsible, caring person, and I know you really love Macey. And I know that he really knows it too."

"Thank you." Julia gave her sister a hug. "But I guess my point is that even though I don't have a child of my own, that experience gave me insight into all of the hard things that parents have to do. I know how carefully Cooper takes care of Macey, and I know it's because he loves her so much. But at some point, he's got to learn to trust, you know? Trust me, and trust that everything will be okay if things start to be different. When Macey starts getting older, that's going to become even more true as she starts to want to make her own decisions. And I think the same applies here. You just need to trust. You raised Samantha to be a responsible, confident young woman and all you can do now is trust that she's learned her lessons well. You know?"

Hazel nodded, feeling a surge of relief. "You're right." She heaved a sigh. "It isn't fair to not trust my daughter. It's not like I'm the only one who can protect her, she can also protect herself. At least to an extent."

"That's the spirit." Julia nodded. "And you can always talk with her about these things before she has to face them, you know? Remind her that she needs to be careful with her heart."

"Good point." Hazel smiled, feeling better already.

"Besides," Julia added with a smirk, "you still have a few more years of having Samantha almost totally under your care. And then she gets to get her driver's license in three years. Won't that be fun?"

Hazel groaned at the thought, which made both sisters erupt into laughter.

"It'll be fine," Julia assured her, chuckling. "Again, she's a smart young woman. She can handle herself. And that's one of the most important parts of growing up—learning that we can make good decisions. But you've got to let her make those decisions in order for her to learn that, you know? Remember how Mom and Dad let us do things? They gave us good advice and they raised us well, but then they gave us a reasonable amount of freedom. That made us all grow up into the truly remarkable adults that we are."

She waved a hand to gesture between the two of them, and Hazel laughed.

"You're right. Thank you, Julia. Thanks for the advice, and also for noticing that I was worried and coming to find me. I appreciate you."

"Of course." Julia gave Hazel another hug, rocking her back and forth a little. "You can always come to me or Alexis or Mom when you're feeling worried. You don't have to face your fears all by yourself."

"That's a good reminder, thank you. It's like I

know that, but sometimes I get so caught up in my own head that I don't think to reach out to you guys. And in this case, I guess I feel kind of silly to be worrying so much about this."

Julia shook her head. "It's not silly. You care about your daughter. We can all relate to feeling worried about someone we love. But just you remember that she's going to be more than fine."

Julia wrapped her arm around Hazel's shoulders and together they walked back to their group. Samantha was just stepping out of the changing room, wearing a darling pale pink dress with a full skirt, and tears sprang into Hazel's eyes.

"You look amazing, honey," she said, hugging her daughter.

"Aw, thanks." Samantha spun around. "I think this might be it. I would love to dance in this dress."

"I can imagine! And it looks like something Glinda might wear," Vivian said, beaming at her granddaughter.

Hazel smiled, knowing her daughter was going to have an amazing time at the dance and that she was well-equipped to take care of her own heart.

# CHAPTER TWENTY-TWO

Dean stood in his office at work, staring at the carpet without seeing it. His brain was spinning, and although he was smiling slightly, his palms were beginning to sweat from nervousness. He wiped them on the pants of his mechanic's jumpsuit, thinking to himself that he couldn't remember the last time his palms had sweated that much.

He glanced at the clock, noting that it had been fifteen minutes since he'd had Keith call Noelle. He wondered if she was just going to come by the auto repair shop, or if she might call him first before bringing her car in.

*Maybe this was a stupid idea,* he thought, scratching the back of his neck. *I should have just called her myself instead of having Keith call her. I guess it just seemed more plausible that way.*

He started to pace, feeling jittery. The truth was that there was nothing wrong with Noelle's car, but he'd asked Keith to call her and tell her that there was a minor adjustment that they'd forgotten to do on it and she needed to bring it in.

Dean had concocted the scheme because he wanted to talk to Noelle in person, and he thought it would be a good way to get her to come over to the shop. He knew that he would see her again soon for physical therapy, but what he wanted to talk to her about was something he didn't feel would be right to bring up in the professional setting of his physical therapy appointments.

He heard the front door of the auto shop jangle, and he hurried over to the door of his office that led to the lobby. He opened it and saw Noelle stepping inside the shop.

"Hey!" She smiled at him, but she looked a little flustered. "Is everything okay?"

"Oh, yeah, definitely. It's nothing to worry about." Dean cleared his throat, wondering more than ever if his scheme had been such a good idea after all.

"What needs to be done on my car?" she asked,

stepping a few paces toward him. "Keith said it was something minor?"

"Uh, yeah, I'll have the guys take a look at it," Dean said awkwardly. "It's probably nothing."

Noelle frowned. She seemed to be slightly guarded and his heart sank a little. Making her uncomfortable was not what he had intended to do at all.

"I guess—well, I'm confused." Noelle exhaled, her expression quizzical. "Why did you just think of this now? It had seemed like you'd done such a thorough job on my car, and I don't understand why something was missed when you were checking it over. You seem like you're very professional here, and well—I mean, I don't mean to be rude, but—I don't understand."

Dean cleared his throat again, realizing he'd made a mess of things.

*I need to just be honest with her,* he thought.

"Noelle, I'm sorry. I didn't think—well, I came up with kind of a silly plan just now and I see that I should have thought it through better before putting it into action."

She cocked her head to one side, clearly unsure of what he was talking about. "What kind of a plan?"

"There's nothing left to do on your car. I

invented that as a pretext for asking you to come over here. I—I wanted to talk to you."

Noelle blinked at him a couple of times and then her eyebrows lifted slowly. "Is everything okay?"

He nodded. "Yeah, everything's okay. I mean, I hope so."

Her brow furrowed even more. "You hope so?"

Dean shook his head and ran his fingers through his hair. "There I go, making a mess of things again. Sorry. Yes! Everything is okay."

"You could have called the office," she said slowly. "I mean, if you needed to talk to me. I'm assuming this is about your physical therapy?"

"Well, it's... it's just that... I wanted to talk to you in person. And I know I could have gone there or waited until our next appointment, but... well, I wanted the conversation to be outside of your office. It's—well, it's personal. It's not something I feel comfortable discussing in a professional setting like that."

Noelle sat down in one of the lobby chairs. "What's going on?" She sounded a little breathless and her eyes were wide.

Dean sat down in the chair across from hers. He clasped his hands and then unclasped them again, unsure of where to begin. "Noelle, I... I would like to be switched to another PT."

She stared at him, and he could tell that she was upset. "I don't understand," she stammered. "I thought you enjoyed working with me. And your progress is fantastic. I mean, Chip is also a wonderful PT, but I can assure you he wouldn't be able to help you along any faster than I've been helping you."

He shook his head. "It's not that."

"Well, why then?"

Dean swallowed, feeling his heart race. He took a deep breath. "I want to be switched so that I can ask you out."

Noelle froze, and her mouth popped open into a perfect little "O" of surprise. For a few moments, neither of them said anything. Dean rolled his shoulders back, worrying that she was about to turn him down. His palms were sweating fiercely again, and he wiped them off on his pants legs.

"Like on a date?" she said finally.

"Yes. I really enjoyed showing you around town," he said, his voice steady despite how nervous he felt. "You're wonderful company. You're kind and fun to be around, and I realized that I wanted to be more than just friends with you. And you're really a wonderful physical therapist. My admiration for you has grown with every session, not only because of your knowledge but also because of what an encouraging, uplifting person you are. And I've been happy being single—I mean, for years. My sisters have been trying to get me to go out with people, and I just haven't felt any kind of a real tug in that direction. Not until you."

Noelle was sitting there staring at him, looking shocked. He didn't know what she was thinking so he nervously continued talking.

"I know it's tricky, since we met in a professional capacity. I'm sure you're not allowed to date your clients, and I wouldn't want to ask you to anyway—I think that would be wrong. But that's why I wanted to switch physical therapists. So that I could ask you out. And I don't want to make you uncomfortable or anything, but I'm wondering if you felt what I felt the other day. When we shared that moment in your office. I felt so attracted to you then, and I still do. Did you feel any of that too? Some measure of attraction toward me?"

Three heart-pounding seconds passed, and then Noelle nodded. Slowly, a smile spread across her face.

"Sorry," she said, pressing a hand to her cheek, which was slightly flushed. "I'm just in such a total daze. Yeah, I did. I definitely am attracted to you too."

"Oh." Dean found himself smiling, and he realized his heart was beating faster than ever. Now, however, instead of nervous he felt absolutely wonderful. "You are?"

"Yeah, I—well, like you were saying. I've been realizing that I'd like to be more than friends with you too. You're great company, and I admire the way you handle your business here."

"Yeah? And for the record, we've never actually forgotten to check something in someone's car and asked them to come back in."

"I didn't think so." She laughed, the sound light and musical. "I was like, 'What on earth is going on? That doesn't seem like him at all.'"

"You should have seen Keith's face when I asked him to call you and tell you that." Dean chuckled too, joining in her laughter. "I think he thought I was pranking him for a second."

"Well, you'll have to tell him that it was all a ruse to try to get me to come here so we could talk in person." Her eyes twinkled at him.

"He'll never let me live it down." He grinned. "Sorry I had you drive over here. And that I made you nervous. It was a silly plan."

She shrugged. "Well, it worked, didn't it?"

"So you'll go out with me? We don't need to be officially dating or anything, but I'd like to switch to Chip so that I can take you out."

"That sounds great. I accept your asking me out."

"Amazing. Do we need to do any kind of fancy paperwork first?"

"Nope." She tapped the side of her head. "Got all the confirmation that you'd like to

switch therapists stored away in here." She smiled at him, and the expression on her face was so sweet that his heart did a somersault. "What's a good day for you?"

"Hm, how about Saturday? In the evening?"

"Sounds perfect." She was grinning just as broadly as he was, and he felt a surge of happiness at the fact that she was clearly excited too. "Saturday it is."

He stood up, knowing that he needed to get back to work and that he shouldn't keep her. Still, he felt reluctant to be parted from her. "You want me to take a look at your car, now that you've brought it all the way down here?"

"No, that's okay." She laughed, standing up as well. "I trust your initial analysis."

For a moment, they stood there smiling at each

other. Dean felt excitement coursing through his body, and he felt more energetic than he had in years.

"I guess I'd better let you get back to work," she said, starting toward the door. "I'll see you on Saturday. Text me the details?"

"I will."

They exchanged one more grin and then she slipped out of the shop. Dean stood in the lobby watching her go for a moment. Then he turned around and headed back to his office, eagerness bubbling inside of him.

# CHAPTER TWENTY-THREE

Hazel took a sip of the lavender tea that she'd made for herself, hoping it would help steady her nerves. She glanced at the clock on the wall in the kitchen, biting her lip. It was just a few more minutes until Samantha was going to leave for the school dance, and all of Hazel's nervousness about the event had returned.

Two days earlier, Samantha had vaulted into the house after returning from school, looking wild with happiness. She'd squealed out the news that Austin had asked her to go to the dance with him. Hazel had been torn between happiness for her daughter and a sudden storm of worries about the event.

She listened to the sound of Samantha's footsteps on the ceiling overhead. Her daughter seemed to be walking more heavily than usual, and in a more rhythmic way.

Hazel chuckled to herself, realizing that Samantha was probably practicing her dancing. Then she imagined Samantha dancing with Austin, and she pressed her lips together.

*I wish I'd gotten a chance to meet him before all this*, she thought, taking a frazzled sip of her tea. *I think she's really too young to be going with a boy. What kind of parents does he have? Are they encouraging this?*

She shook her head. When Samantha had told her that Austin had asked her—describing the scene in minute detail, gushing over the way he'd approached her in front of her locker and handed her a card that said, *Will you go to the dance with me?*—Hazel had considered telling her daughter that she was too young to go with a boy, and she would have to just spend time with Austin at the dance, not go officially as his date.

But the ecstatic happiness of her daughter had convinced her not to do that, at least not during their initial conversation.

Afterward, she'd wrestled with the idea. She'd worried that she should have put her foot down right away or told Samantha weeks ago that she was too young to go with a boy.

But the more she thought about it, the more she remembered Julia's advice that she needed to trust her daughter to make smart decisions. She didn't want to push Samantha away by holding onto the leash too tightly. She knew how much it meant to her daughter that Austin had asked her to the dance, and she knew that she would be crushed if she had to tell him that she wasn't going with him after all. Besides, there would be chaperones at the dance, and Samantha was a good kid going with a boy who sounded like he was a good kid too.

Hazel drank more of her tea, staring into space and wondering when Samantha was going to come downstairs. They'd spent the last hour together, getting her ready. Samantha had put on the pink dress that they'd found with the rest of the Owens women, and she looked as pretty as a picture in it.

Her cheeks were so flushed and her eyes were sparkling so much that she didn't need makeup, even if Hazel would have allowed her to wear it. They'd found a pair of low pink heels to wear with the dress, and they matched it perfectly. Hazel's heart had given a bittersweet pang when she'd seen her daughter wearing heels for the first time. Samantha had been practicing walking in them almost non-stop since they'd been purchased.

Hazel glanced at the clock again. "You'd better come downstairs in a minute, honey!" she called. "It's almost time to go!"

"Okay!" Samantha called.

At that moment, the doorbell rang. Hazel's heart jumped up, wondering if it was Austin and his parents arriving. Samantha had told her that they'd offered to come pick her up, since Austin wasn't old enough to drive yet.

She hurried through the living room to the front door and yanked it open. Instead of three strangers, however, she saw Julia standing there.

"Hey!" Hazel pulled her sister into a hug. "Thanks for coming over."

"I figured you could use the company." Julia smiled sympathetically. "I know you're nervous about this whole thing."

"Oh, gosh." Hazel let out a long sigh. "I'm trying not to be, but you're right, I am. Were we this into boys at her age?"

"Alexis was." Julia laughed. "And I think I kind of was too. I don't think you were until you were older, but you'd be the best person to answer that."

"I honestly don't remember." Hazel ran her

fingers through her hair. "It's all become kind of a blur."

"I hear that." Julia stepped inside. "How are you doing?"

"Jittery. Drinking lavender tea." Hazel laughed.

"Oh, really? Could I have some too? That sounds delicious."

"You got it." Hazel felt glad to have a task to do. "Come on into the kitchen and I'll make you a cup."

Julia followed Hazel into the cozy little kitchen. "So you're nervous. Tell me about what's making you nervous."

"I just—I just have some misgivings, I guess. She seems so young to be going to a dance with a boy. But I know I have to let the reins go a bit so that Samantha doesn't feel stifled and resent me."

"Oh, I don't think she'd ever resent you. I think she's empathetic enough to understand where you'd be coming from, even if you did choose to be that strict."

Hazel shook her head. "She couldn't be, not really. She can't understand why I'm afraid the way another adult could understand it. When she thinks about boys, all she sees is happily ever after. Until you get your heart broken, you think you're invincible."

Julia hugged her sister sideways. "I see what you mean. But I think you're going to be able to find a healthy balance. Trust your instincts. No one is a perfect parent, and all you can do is your best. Talk to Samantha about your concerns, but also let her explore and have the adventures she wants to have. She's got to learn to navigate the world on her own, and that training is starting now."

Hazel groaned. "Oh, you're right. I wish it wasn't starting for another five—no, ten—years."

Julia chuckled. "Just let her have fun today and let yourself have fun too. There's nothing to worry about. She's just going to a fun dance with a nice boy."

"Yes." Hazel smiled. "A fun dance with a nice boy. And I'm glad she's so excited, I really am."

"Speaking of Glinda the Good, where is she? Shouldn't she be downstairs by now?"

"She should." Hazel glanced toward the staircase with a chuckle. "She's probably twirling around again. I would be too, if I was her age and I was wearing a dress with a skirt like that." She started toward the staircase, intending to go up it and remind Samantha that it was nearly time to go.

At that moment, however, the doorbell rang again.

"Oh, that must be the boy and his parents," she said, feeling suddenly flustered again.

"Don't be nervous!" Julia called after her, laughing a little, as Hazel hurried over to the front door.

She opened it, but to her surprise, Samantha's best friends, Willow and Natalie, were standing on the doorstep. Both girls were clearly ready for the dance—Willow was wearing the Wicked Witch inspired outfit that Samantha had described, and Natalie was wearing a beautiful silver dress.

"Hey, girls!" Both of Samantha's best friends were great kids, and Hazel was always happy to see them. "What are you doing here?"

"We're here to pick Samantha up," Willow said, grinning from ear to ear. "My mom's over there in the car waiting for us."

Hazel's lips parted, and she felt a flop of worry that Samantha had forgotten to tell her friends about her plans with Austin. She didn't want Willow or Natalie to feel badly that Samantha wasn't going to the dance with them. She decided not to say anything yet, however. It was possible that Samantha's carpooling plans had changed and she just hadn't told her mother yet.

"She's almost ready," Hazel said, smiling. "Why don't you two come inside for a moment?"

The girls stepped into the house just as Samantha was coming down the stairs. The moment she saw her friends, Samantha squealed with delight and raced to hug them.

"You guys made it! I thought you were going to be late!"

"No, my mom drives even faster than my dad does," Willow said, shaking her head as if she was wondering how she would ever get her mother to behave properly.

Julia and Hazel exchanged a quizzical glance over the girls' heads.

"Hey, honey," Hazel said quietly to her daughter. "What about Austin? I thought you were going with him?" She pressed her lips together, worrying that Austin had changed his mind and Samantha was already dealing with the pain of rejection.

"I'll see him there." Samantha was grinning, clearly not upset in any way. "And I promised to dance with him—"

"Ooh!" her friends squealed.

"—but I decided that I wanted to go the dance with 'The Rosebuds.'" She said the name with infinite pride, and then all three of the girls struck dramatic poses.

Julia and Hazel exchanged another glance, both of them clearly trying not to laugh.

"What are 'The Rosebuds'?" Hazel asked.

Samantha's eyes danced mischievously. "Mom, Aunt Julia, take a seat on the couch for a second."

"My goodness, this is exciting," Julia said.

Hazel sat down beside her sister, feeling both delighted and extremely relieved. Samantha wasn't nearly as boy-crazy as she'd thought. If she was choosing her friends over being chosen by a boy, that was setting a healthy pattern for her future. It was clear that Samantha didn't think she needed a boy to complete her, she was perfectly happy to be her full self with her friends.

"Ladies and—ladies!" Samantha began to speak in a dramatic announcer voice. "Thank you for coming to the concert of 'The Rosebuds,' the best girl band in Rosewood Beach!"

Samantha and her friends began to sing a popular pop song, going back and forth from solos to group singing and changing up which one of them was singing as a soloist every few lines. They were giggling a great deal and some of their pitches were a little flat, but they all performed with gusto and an impressive amount of confidence.

As soon as their final note ended, Hazel and Julia burst into applause.

"Amazing!" Hazel said, grinning. "You girls sound great together. How long have you wanted to be a band?"

"Uh, a couple of days?" Willow glanced at her friends, frowning a little in concentration.

"'The Rosebuds' are a new band, but we are committed to it." Samantha nodded emphatically, her eyes shining. "We're going to rehearse every Tuesday night for a couple of hours."

"Yeah, in my garage," Natalie said. "Because real bands rehearse in garages."

"Sounds fantastic." Julia grinned. "I'd ask for an encore, but we don't want to keep your mother waiting too long, Willow. And besides, you girls don't want to be late for the dance."

"You're right!" Samantha ran to her mother and hugged her tightly. "Bye, Mom! Love you. I'll see you later!"

"Have an amazing time!"

The girls vaulted out of the house, and Julia and Hazel watched them go from the windows, smiling over how cute the girls looked in their beautiful dresses.

"Oh, well, that's a relief," Hazel said with a big sigh as she watched Samantha hop into Willow's mom's van.

Julia laughed. "I guess that crush was short-lived! Girls her age are into something one minute and then off to something else the next."

"Clearly." Hazel chuckled. "And I'm so glad that she's more excited about having fun with her friends than going to a dance with a boy."

"You seem to be in the clear for now. Sorry you had all that worrying for nothing."

"Oh, I don't think it was for nothing." Hazel shook her head. "This way, I'll feel more prepared when boys inevitably come back around someday. But this was my first test in practicing letting go. Hopefully next time it won't feel so hard."

"Hopefully." Julia nodded sympathetically. "And at least now you know that it's coming."

"And when it does come, I'll be more ready to trust my daughter and let her make her own choices." Hazel smiled. "I can't help hoping she'll be a little older the next time she gets this excited about a boy, but however old she is, I'm going to remind myself that she's smart enough to make her own choices about some things."

# CHAPTER TWENTY-FOUR

Noelle parked her car outside Dean's auto repair shop, her heart thumping in her chest.

*He asked me out. He asked me out*, she thought. *I'm going on a date with Dean. An actual date.*

A grin spread across her face. Ever since Dean had asked her out, she'd felt as though she was living in some kind of pink haze. She'd found herself singing in the shower or while she was doing the dishes. She felt buoyant and eager, and she'd started to count the hours until their date. Now that it had arrived, she was almost bursting with excitement.

She'd put on a cute outfit of dark jeans, light blue heels with a strap, and a pink blazer over a white sweater. She'd done her hair and makeup carefully, applying a pink lipstick and creamy brown eyeshadow. Before leaving her house, she'd turned back and forth in front of her mirror several times, giving herself a pep talk as anticipation bubbled inside her.

Now that she'd arrived at the auto repair shop, she felt nervous, but her eagerness was much stronger than her jitters. She got out of her car, grabbing her small purse and slinging it over her shoulder as she walked up to the front door of the shop.

She'd found it a bit odd when Dean had texted her earlier in the day and asked her if she would meet him at the shop for their date. He'd told her that he would be working, but they could start their date there and he could drive her to dinner in his car.

She glanced at the parking lot of the shop, noting that the only car there was Dean's. She realized he must be working late on some kind of special repair, since all of his employees had already gone home for the day. She pictured him wearing his dirty mechanic jumpsuit, his hands covered in grease, and she smiled to herself. Even if he didn't get a chance to get cleaned up before their dinner, she knew that she would take him even covered in car grease.

She pulled open the door of the repair shop, and a

moment later she stopped in her tracks. Dean was standing in the lobby grinning at her. He wasn't dirty or wearing a mechanic's uniform at all—he was wearing an attractive navy sweater, dark slacks, and dress shoes. His unruly hair had been combed back, making it seem as though he'd really dressed up for the occasion.

"Good evening," he said, his eyes warm. His tone was gentle and familiar, and she felt as though she'd known him for years. "You look amazing."

"Thank you." Her own voice was a little breathless. "So do you. I really like that sweater."

They gave each other a slightly hesitant hug. She would have liked to give him a big squeeze, but she didn't know what the protocol was for a first date—even if the man you were going out with was someone who was already your friend.

"Thanks. I knew it would be chilly tonight. I've got my leather jacket in my car if you end up being cold."

She smiled, loving the idea of getting to wear his jacket. "Should we go?" She took a couple of steps toward the front door.

He shook his head. "I have something to show you first."

"You do, huh?" She smiled, liking the way his

eyes were gleaming almost mischievously. "What is it?"

"You've just got to see it. Come on."

Curious, she followed him into the garage of the shop.

"Am I allowed in here?" she teased. "I thought it was against company policy for customers to be in the garage."

He turned around and winked at her. "But you're not a customer right now."

"Oh, I see." She laughed.

The garage was dimly lit, but she could see well enough to avoid tripping over anything. When they were about halfway across the room, Dean paused at a light switch panel.

"Are you ready?" he asked.

"Ready for what?"

"Nope, answer the question."

"Okay, Mr. Mysterious. Yes, I'm ready."

Dean flipped on the light switches and the garage was flooded with light. At the far end of the room was a car, and Noelle gasped when she saw it.

"Is that... is that a 1988 Porsche 911?" She hurried over to it, thrilled. "It is, isn't it? I didn't know you had one of these here. This is the exact year and make of the car that I worked on with my grandfather."

Dean was beaming at her. "The one you never got to ride in, right?"

She turned back to him, suddenly realizing what was going on. "Did you fix up this car?"

He nodded. "Thanks to PT, my energy levels have gotten so much better, and I'm able to maintain strength in my hands for much longer. That's allowed me to get back to my favorite hobby, restoring cars."

"Dean, that's wonderful." She felt tears springing into her eyes. "I'm so happy for you. Really, that's such great news."

"It is. And I'm really grateful for all your help."

She shook her head. "I was just doing my job. You did this for yourself by putting in the effort. I'm so excited for you." Excited wasn't even a strong enough word—she felt overjoyed.

"Come on and look at it," Dean said, suddenly hurrying toward the car as if he was a kid who couldn't wait to show it to her anymore. "It's just gorgeous. I can't wait to show you how it runs."

"You got it running?" She felt as excited as he looked.

"Oh, yeah, it runs beautifully."

"How long have you had it? I'm surprised you didn't mention it when I brought up the Porsche that my grandmother and I fixed up."

Dean shook his head, smiling. "I didn't mention it because I didn't have it then. I just got it a little while ago from a friend. I—well, I got the idea to fix it up so that you could ride in it. I mean, because you never got to ride in the one that you and your grandfather fixed up."

She stared at him, her heart thumping. "Dean... you fixed this up for me?"

He nodded, smiling almost shyly. "I mean, it was for me too. I enjoyed it. But... well yeah."

She bounded across the garage and gave him a massive hug, squeezing him even tighter than she'd wanted to earlier. "Thank you! This is... I don't even have the words. This is amazing."

"You're so welcome. I thought it would be a great way to show you that... well, I would like to do things for you, Noelle. I'd like to help you out and make sure you have the things you need, and things that make you happy. I like being around you, and I know tonight is only our first date, but I hope things continue with us."

They stood in the garage smiling at each other.

She felt her heart fluttering in her chest like a bird that wanted to fly. "I hope so too."

Neither of them said anything for a few more moments, and then Dean grinned.

"You want to come on a drive with me?"

"Yes!" she almost squealed. "Oh my gosh, yes please."

Dean helped her into the passenger side of the car, and she liked that he was acting like such a gentleman. She found it gracious and endearing. He hurried around to the other side of the car and got into the driver's seat.

"Are you going to be too cold with the top down?" he asked her.

She shook her head. "Even if I am, it'll be worth it. Besides, didn't you offer me a jacket earlier?"

"I did." He grinned. "It's behind your seat there. Put it on whenever you feel like it."

He started the engine, and they exchanged a look of excitement. Using a remote control, he opened the door of the garage and drove the Porsche through it.

"Where do you want to go?" he asked her.

"Anywhere," she said, almost breathless. "I just want to spend some time in this car."

*With you,* she thought. *I think I'd go anywhere with you.*

"Perfect. Wherever the wind may take us." He chuckled. "My favorite kind of driving."

He drove the car along Rosewood Beach's Main Street for a while, and they waved at people they knew. The lights of shops and restaurants were glowing warmly in the dusk, and appetizing smells wafted through the air. Noelle's stomach grumbled, and she knew that dinner was going to taste particularly good when they got around to eating it.

But first, they had driving to do.

Dean took the car farther and farther away from the heart of town, out toward the roads that led along the coast. It was a beautiful night, and as soon as the sun finished setting, the stars came out overhead, speckling the sky like diamonds.

"Such a beautiful car," she murmured, tracing her finger along the edge of her open window. "That engine sounds great."

"Oh, man." He laughed. "I don't think I can handle this. You're beautiful and you're kind and you say things like, 'That engine sounds great.'"

She laughed, feeling thrilled that he'd called her beautiful. "Well, it does. And this night is incredible. It's not too cold, and it smells all spicy like autumn always does." In the next moment, she shivered as a gust of wind rushed over the car.

"Not too cold, huh?" he teased, noticing her shiver.

"Well, not until this moment." She grinned and reached around behind her for Dean's jacket. She slid it on, noticing that it smelled like him, a kind of warm, musky smell. She took a deep breath, enjoying the feeling of no longer being cold and wearing the jacket of the man she had such a crush on.

"You look great in my jacket," he said, glancing at her as he drove.

She smiled. "It's a great jacket."

For a few moments, they were both quiet, but they kept stealing glances at each other and smiling. The stars twinkled overhead and the fragrant wind rushed at their faces. Noelle felt a mixture of excitement and peace that was wonderful, and not like anything she'd ever experienced before.

Unexpectedly, Dean turned the car to the left and started to drive it down an unmarked road.

"What's through here?" Noelle asked, glancing up at the pine trees that had suddenly darkened the road.

"You'll see." He smiled at her and then turned to face the road as he navigated the car through difficult twists and turns. They seemed to be going deeper into a forest, and Noelle listened intently to the sound of owls hooting and the wind sighing in the pine branches.

Then, all at once, the road opened up to a breathtaking overlook. There was a small parking lot just in front of an old stone wall. Beyond the wall was a sheer drop and a magnificent view of the ocean.

"Oh, Dean," she breathed. "This is wonderful."

"I thought you'd like it." He looked as pleased as if he'd made it himself. He parked the car just at the edge of the wall and they sat quietly together for a while, watching the moon light up the tossing waves with flecks of silver.

Her heart was full as she sat there beside him. She was beginning to get hungry, but she didn't want to suggest that they turn around and leave. They seemed to be in the midst of some kind of enchanted moment together, and she didn't want it to end.

"Noelle?"

"Yes, Dean?" She turned to him with a smile, her voice as soft as his.

"I... when I first got my diagnosis, I was devastated. It was a huge blow. I didn't understand why something so bad had happened to me. And I know there's still a lot I need to learn how to deal

with, but now I'm happy that everything worked out
the way that it did."

"Because it made you stronger?"

"Because it led me to meeting you."

Her heart did a somersault. "Oh. I—"

She didn't know what to say, and it didn't matter.
In the next moment, Dean leaned his face in toward
hers and gently kissed her.

"I'm so happy that everything led you to me,
Dean," she whispered. "Even though I wish you
didn't have to deal with your diagnosis. And I'm so
happy my path led me here to Rosewood Beach."

"It feels like it was meant to be, doesn't it?"

"It does."

They shared a smile and then they shared
another kiss. Then Dean's stomach growled loudly
and they both burst out laughing.

"Time for dinner, I guess." Dean chortled.
"What do you think? Should we go out exploring in a
neighboring town, or do you want to go back to
Rosewood Beach for dinner?"

She considered it for a moment. "Rosewood
Beach. There are quite a few restaurants there I
haven't tried yet, and I'd like to. And besides, you're
so good at helping me get to know our town."

"Rosewood Beach it is," he said. "Sounds great to me."

He turned the car around and they headed back toward Rosewood Beach. For a few minutes, they drove in silence, both of them seeming to be in a kind of daze. Noelle felt as though her whole body was glowing with happiness. She glanced over at Dean, wanting to look at him to convince herself she wasn't dreaming.

He reached over and took her hand in his.

"Yes?" he asked, smiling.

She nodded. "Yes."

They talked on and off as they drove back to the twinkling lights of Rosewood Beach. Sometimes they sat quietly and enjoyed the sights and smells of the beautiful evening. Sometimes they chatted about things they both felt excited about. The entire drive back, Dean never once let go of her hand.

# CHAPTER TWENTY-FIVE

Alexis smiled as she watched the early morning sunlight flicker across the countertops of her and Grayson's kitchen. It was a beautiful Sunday morning, and through the window she could see the leaves of the trees flickering in the wind. The sunlight was making their vibrant shades of red, orange, and yellow even more resplendent, and for a moment she paused to stare at the beautiful sight.

A yawn overtook her, and she stretched, thinking to herself that it was nice to have the day off from work.

*Maybe Grayson and I could go for a walk later,* she thought. *I'd love to enjoy this beautiful weather. I know it's supposed to be chilly today, but nothing a warm sweater wouldn't take care of.*

She began to hum quietly as she opened the cupboards and took out a bag of coffee grounds. She scooped some into a coffee filter, inhaling the rich, nutty aroma with a sigh of pleasure. She loved the smell of coffee, and soon the coffee maker was gurgling cheerfully, filling the kitchen with the scent.

She turned on the radio, and the soothing sounds of jazz poured out of it. She glanced upstairs as she heard the sound of a door closing. When she had first come downstairs to the kitchen, Grayson had been sitting at the kitchen table working, but then he had gone back upstairs for a while. She smiled. She liked listening to the sound of him moving around their house—it was a comfortable sound that made her feel safe.

She walked across the kitchen to the windows behind the kitchen table. She opened one of them and took a deep breath of the fragrant garden air. It was as chilly as she'd thought it would be, so she didn't leave the window open, but she liked to smell the fresh air and the lingering sweet smells of the garden.

After she'd shut the window and was turning back to the main part of the kitchen, she noticed Grayson's laptop sitting open at the table. The screen was facing the wall, and she hadn't been able to see it while she was busy making the coffee.

The screen showed what looked like a website that was in the process of being made. The colors of it were beautiful—deep purple, sage, white, and navy. She squinted at the screen in confusion, wondering why Grayson would be putting together a website, especially a website that was constructed with such feminine colors.

At that moment, Grayson stepped into the kitchen. He saw Alexis looking at his laptop screen and hurried across the room.

"Let me just close that up," he said, smiling briskly but looking flustered. He shut the laptop and swiftly tucked it under his arm.

"What are you up to?" she asked, her suspicions aroused by his behavior.

"Nothing." He hurried over to the doorway that led into the living room and went through it. He set his laptop down on the coffee table and returned a few seconds later. "What are we making for breakfast? I was thinking blueberry pancakes, what do you think?" He wrapped his arms around her and gave her a big kiss.

"Oh, no," she said. "You're not changing the

subject that easily, mister. What's going on? Why are you acting so oddly about your laptop?"

"It's just something for work." Grayson stuck his head in the refrigerator and began to rummage around. "We do have blueberries, don't we? I was sure I saw some in here the other day."

"Those were unusual colors for a finance company to be using, weren't they? Don't businesses usually operate using more neutral colors?"

"Oh, not all the time." Grayson's voice was muffled because his head was stuck so far inside the refrigerator.

"I've never seen such a pretty business website before. That purple was really kind of a feminine color, wasn't it?"

"There's navy too. And sage."

"Sure, but with the purple?"

"It's just a website, not any kind of a big deal."

She took him by the shoulders and gently yanked him back out of the fridge. "Grayson, I can tell you're hiding something from me. I've never seen you burrow so far into the refrigerator before. You'd think you were trying to live in it or something. Come on. Tell me."

He let out a long sigh. "It was supposed to be a surprise. I wanted to surprise you."

She frowned, confused. "Surprise me with what?"

"Okay, come here." He took her hand and led her into the living room. He sat down on the couch and she sat down beside him, wondering what he was about to show her. He opened his laptop, revealing the website page that she'd gotten a glimpse of before.

"What you saw was a fairly unfinished page, but I've got most of the website basically ready to go." He clicked a couple of times, revealing a gorgeous home page. Across the top was a banner that read, "Designer Jewelry by Alexis Bennett."

She gasped, clapping her hands to her mouth. "You—what—oh, Grayson, this is absolutely beautiful."

He grinned, looking thrilled. "Do you like it? I know dark purple is your favorite color, and I wanted it to look like something that goes along with the color schemes you often use for your jewelry. I've been taking pictures of the pieces you've already made, and there's a gallery page... here."

He clicked again, revealing a beautiful page that featured several of her best jewelry designs. "So this page here is just to show people what you make. But if they click any of these links, here or here, it takes them to this page where they can order any of your pieces."

Alexis leaned forward, feeling in awe of what she was looking at. Seeing her work portrayed in such a professional way made her feel significantly more confident in herself. Her jewelry really did look incredible. Grayson had been able to see that even when she couldn't, and he'd believed in her. Now, her dream was about to become a reality because of the faith he had in her and her work.

"Thank you." She took his face in her hands and kissed him. "This is... I don't even have words, really. This shows me how much you care about me. It's really wonderful. Thank you so much."

"I do care about you." He set the laptop down and wrapped his arms around her. "These are the kinds of things I do well, so of course I'm going to do them for my favorite person. I want to make sure that you have the head start you need to make your dream become a reality."

"I wouldn't even have dreamed of trying to sell my jewelry like this if it weren't for you. You believed in me and made all this possible. Thank you so much, sweetheart."

"Of course."

For a while, they sat there with their arms

around each other, and Alexis felt a surge of happiness.

"You want to see the rest of it?" Grayson sounded almost as eager as a schoolboy wanting to show off. "I've put in some cool things I want to show you."

"Absolutely." She laughed and nuzzled his nose.

He opened his laptop again and began to show her the website in more detail. "See here, the home page immediately gives a potential buyer a sense of the different kinds of pieces you offer. There's pictures of earrings, bracelets, and necklaces, and this side bar here makes it easy to click on the sale galleries. And then once you have reviews, those will go right here, immediately showing people how well-respected your work is."

"If I get any good reviews." She wrinkled her nose.

"Oh, you will. And see how I've tried to organize everything with buyer intent in mind? This set-up should promote maximum sales. I know you're going to succeed at this, sweetheart."

She felt tears spring into her eyes. "I'm so touched, Grayson. Why does this mean so much to you?"

He looked into her eyes. "You spent so many

years supporting my ventures, especially when I was just getting started, and I want to do the same for you."

She squeezed his hand, feeling overwhelmed. "Thank you, sweetheart. You're so good at all this stuff, and I couldn't do it without you."

"Oh, I don't know about that." He smiled at her. "But I'm happy to support you the way you've supported me. I think that's such a big part of what marriage is about—supporting and encouraging each other's dreams. I want you to be able to have a job that brings you joy."

"It sounds incredible. I would love to do what I love for a living."

He leaned over and kissed her cheek. "I'm excited to see all of this start to gain traction. It's going to be a rollercoaster, but in a good way."

"I can't wait. And speaking of supporting each other's dreams, I believe you mentioned something about blueberry pancakes?"

"I did. You want to make some blueberry pancakes with me?"

"Yes, I do. With scrambled eggs and bacon on the side."

"Did you hear my stomach grumble as soon as you said the word 'bacon'?" He laughed. "Come on, let's get to it." Grayson stood and helped Alexis to her feet.

They went into the kitchen together and began to prepare breakfast. As they worked, Alexis kept thinking about the beautiful website her husband had made for her and feeling eager for the future.

# CHAPTER TWENTY-SIX

Dean stepped up to The Lighthouse Grill, taking a deep breath of the familiar savory smells of clam chowder and French fries. He opened the front door and was immediately greeted by the sound of a few customers talking and laughing, and of cutlery clinking. For the most part, however, the pub was fairly quiet. It was before the lunch rush, and as he glanced around the room, he didn't see anyone who could help him with the to-go lunch that he'd ordered for himself and Noelle.

"Huh," he muttered.

He glanced around the dining room, noting that he didn't even see any wait staff walking around. He concluded that everyone must be on their break because the pub was so quiet at the moment.

He wandered into the kitchen and found that empty as well. He felt a little surprised, since there was usually at least someone in the kitchen, but it was clear that the chefs had been cooking only a few minutes ago, since the kitchen was filled with fresh aromas of food.

He made his way along the back hallway toward the office, the door of which was ajar. He peered through it and grinned when he saw Alexis sitting at the computer.

"Excuse me, Ma'am, is this place open for business?" he teased, stepping inside the office. "You'd think a person would be able to get a meal at a restaurant. Why is the staff slacking?"

Alexis looked up with a grin. She waved her hand through the air, dismissing his teasing. "Everyone's on a break right now. We're always really slow at this time, although it'll pick up again in about twenty minutes."

"Wow, you've got it down to a science, don't you?"

She laughed. "Barring the occasional busload of tourists or teams of kids passing through because of a sports game, our customer base is a pretty consistent group of people. Rosewood Beach's folks know what they want and when they want it."

Dean chuckled. "Yeah, that sounds about right. But I'm here for some—" He paused, noticing his sister looking at the computer again with a radiant expression. Clearly, something on the screen was making her very happy.

"What's up with you?" he asked, stepping toward her. "You're glowing."

"Come and look at this," she said eagerly, scooting her swivel chair to the side to make room for him to stand next to her.

He peered down at the computer screen and saw a retail website listing.

"Hmm, what am I looking at?"

Alexis clicked a couple of times, revealing a beautiful website featuring pictures of jewelry. "You are looking at the website of Rosewood Beach's first resident jewelry maker."

"Wow, that's really cool. Who's Rosewood Beach's first—hey, aren't those the earrings you made? Alexis! Is this your website?"

"Ta da!" She laughed, her eyes bright with excitement. "Grayson helped me with the website. Well, actually, he made it. Doesn't it look amazing?"

"It does." Dean leaned forward, feeling impressed. "But it's not as great as your jewelry pieces. Look at those! You're going to get sales for sure."

"I have sales already!" she practically squealed. "Grayson kept telling me this was going to work, and now I actually believe him."

"I'm not surprised at all. Congratulations, Alexis!" He reached down and gave her a big hug. "This is amazing."

"Thank you! Now, what were you saying about needing service?"

He grinned. "Yeah, I put in a to-go order. Is it ready yet?"

"Oh, it should be. The cooks wouldn't go on a break if there was still a to-go order that needed to be done."

She stood up and went out into the kitchen. He followed her and watched as she hurried over to a metal shelving unit.

"Here it is." She held up a white plastic bag that was bulky with the to-go containers inside. A receipt was stapled to the outside of the bag, and she glanced over it. "A Reuben with mashed potatoes on the side? Isn't that Noelle's favorite?"

Dean shrugged. "Maybe. Maybe I ordered both the tuna melt and the Reuben because I'm extremely hungry."

She swatted his arm playfully. "Oh, stop. I know it's for Noelle. You two have a date this afternoon?"

"Yeah, we do." He couldn't help grinning. "I'm on my way over to the physical therapy office to meet her."

"Sounds lovely. How are things going with you two?" Her eyes widened mischievously, and Dean laughed, knowing how thrilled she must be about his new relationship considering how long she'd tried to get him to date one of the women of Rosewood Beach.

"Super well." His heart stirred just thinking about Noelle. She always brightened his day, and he found himself thinking about her and the conversations they had a great deal of the time.

"I'm really happy to hear that. So you're planning on staying together, huh?"

"I guess we'll just have to wait and see." Dean smiled, and he knew his happiness was clearly painted on his face, allowing Alexis to see that his chances with Noelle were definitely favorable.

"Well, I don't want to keep you." She gave him a hug. "You have a great date, and I'll talk to you later!"

"Talk to you later! I look forward to being interrogated."

"Oh, shush!"

He left the kitchen with an impish grin on his face, wanting to make sure he left before Alexis had a chance to throw something at him.

He stepped outside into the sunlight and took a deep breath of the crisp autumn air. It was chillier than it had been when he'd first started dating Noelle a few weeks earlier, but with a jacket and a warm knit hat on, he felt comfortable.

He walked toward the physical therapy office, the bag of to-go food swinging in his right hand. He could smell the delicious food as he walked, and he was looking forward to eating it. Even more than that, however, he was looking forward to seeing Noelle.

He reached the cheerful little physical therapy office and stepped inside. The familiar sight of the lobby greeted him, and he smiled as he noticed the cute and quirky Halloween decorations that had been set up around the room. He had a feeling that Noelle had picked them out, and he made a mental note to ask her about them later. His favorite was a sparkling pumpkin sporting a happy expression and a purple top hat.

Noelle stepped out of her office, and his heart skipped a beat as soon as he saw her. He was amazed that butterflies still kicked up in his stomach every time he set eyes on her.

"Hey." She perked up at the sight of him, hurrying across the lobby toward him.

She gave him a big hug, and he squeezed her tightly. She was wearing a large fleece sweatshirt and a pink hat with a pom-pom on the top. He thought she looked absolutely adorable.

"Hey, you," he murmured. "How's work going today so far?"

"Oh, great," she answered as they separated. "I still miss working with my favorite client, but everyone else is lovely too." She chuckled.

"Well, here's the question. Would you rather work with your favorite client or go eat an amazing picnic lunch with your favorite client?"

"Oh, well, when you put it like that, definitely the lunch."

They both laughed and stepped out of the physical therapy office together. A brisk wind rushed against their faces, and Noelle's cheeks were soon rosy.

"Where to?" he asked her as they strolled along the sidewalk together hand-in-hand. "Somewhere outside, right?"

She nodded. "Thanks for being the kind of guy who will go on a picnic with me in the middle of autumn."

"Hey, it's a beautiful day. And I love autumn."

"After we're done eating, we should pick up some pumpkin spice cookies from Seaside Sweets Bakery."

Dean nodded immediately, loving the idea, and she giggled at him. "Yes please."

"My treat, since you bought lunch."

"No, I can—"

"Shh." She held up a finger. "My treat."

He chuckled. "Yes, ma'am."

"Oh look, the town square!" she said eagerly. "Let's eat in the gazebo. It looks so cozy surrounded by all these beautiful colored trees."

They sat down inside the gazebo and began to eat their meals. The food wasn't quite hot anymore, but it was still satisfyingly warm and delicious. They ate quietly for a while, savoring their first few bites, and then they began to joke and talk.

As he watched her laughing over a silly comment he'd made about a passing car, he felt his heart stir with an ache of hopefulness. He was feeling more and more that he wanted to officially be her boyfriend, but he didn't want to move too quickly. He wasn't sure how to bring up the subject with her, but he knew it was something that he wanted to discuss with her sooner rather than later. He felt ready to take the next step and make their relationship official and exclusive, but he didn't know if she felt the same way or not.

"Thanks for bringing my favorite lunch." She smiled at him, almost shyly. "I love that I didn't have to tell you what to order for me. You remember what my likes and dislikes are. That makes me feel really special."

"I'm glad." The words, "That's because you're very special to me" were on the tip of his tongue, but he wasn't sure if he should say them out loud or not. He didn't know if that would be too forward.

"And you've done so many sweet things for me. Like how you went out of your way to restore that Porsche. You did that for me, and it was so special. The things you do... well, they're the kinds of things a boyfriend would do." She looked right into his eyes as she said the words, her expression eager and hopeful.

Dean realized that his heart was suddenly racing. "What are you saying?" he asked softly, looking into her eyes.

She grinned. "Well, I was wondering if you'd like to make us official. Be exclusive. Be my boyfriend."

Dean's eyes widened, and he felt a smile spread across his face. "Yeah? You want to?"

She nodded. "I really do. I think we really have something here. Even before we were dating, we had something, I think. As much as I tried to tell myself that we were just friends, I couldn't do it. There was always a spark. And that makes me feel really good about us. I can see this working out. So... do you want to?"

"Yes please!" He was grinning from ear to ear. "I've been wanting to ask you—I keep thinking about it—but I wasn't sure if it was too early or not. I didn't want to rush you."

"I hear what you're saying. But I think all relationships have a different pace and this is ours. It helps that we started out as friends, I think. We got a clear picture of who we are as people before we actually started dating."

He nodded. "Yes. Definitely. You already know how cheesy all my jokes are."

"And I love them!"

He laughed and wrapped his arms around her. "So we're official?"

"Officially official. Hi, boyfriend."

"Hi, girlfriend."

His heart stirred with a deep happiness as he leaned his head forward and kissed her.

ALSO BY FIONA BAKER

**The Marigold Island Series**

The Beachside Inn

Beachside Beginnings

Beachside Promises

Beachside Secrets

Beachside Memories

Beachside Weddings

Beachside Holidays

Beachside Treasures

**The Sea Breeze Cove Series**

The House by the Shore

A Season of Second Chances

A Secret in the Tides

The Promise of Forever

A Haven in the Cove

The Blessing of Tomorrow

A Memory of Moonlight

**The Saltwater Sunsets Series**

Whale Harbor Dreams

Whale Harbor Sisters

Whale Harbor Reunions

Whale Harbor Horizons

Whale Harbor Vows

Whale Harbor Blooms

Whale Harbor Adventures

Whale Harbor Blessings

**The Rosewood Beach Series**

Return to Rosewood Beach

Sea Glass Serenade

A Place for Daydreams

A Bright Winter Season

Moonlit Harbor Nights

Where Sea Meets Sky

A New Chapter in Rosewood Beach

Wishes at Water's Edge

A Breeze over Rosewood Beach

Under the Lighthouse Glow

Autumn by the Seashore

Footsteps in the Sand

**Evergreen Hollow Christmas**

The Inn at Evergreen Hollow

Snowflakes and Surprises

A Christmas to Remember

Mistletoe and Memories

A Season of Magic

**The Snowy Pine Ridge Series**

The Christmas Lodge

Sweet Christmas Wish

Second Chance Christmas

Christmas at the Guest House

A Cozy Christmas Escape

The Christmas Reunion

**For a full list of my books and series, visit my website at** www.fionabakerauthor.com!

# ABOUT THE AUTHOR

Fiona writes sweet, feel-good contemporary women's fiction and family sagas with a bit of romance.

She hopes her characters will start to feel like old friends as you follow them on their journeys of love, family, friendship, and new beginnings. Her heartwarming storylines and charming small-town beach settings are a particular favorite of readers.

When she's not writing, she loves eating good meals with friends, trying out new recipes, and finding the perfect glass of wine to pair them with. She lives on the East Coast with her husband and their two trouble-making dogs.

Follow her on her website, Facebook, or Bookbub.

Sign up to receive her newsletter, where you'll get free books, exclusive bonus content, and info on her new releases and sales!

Made in United States
Cleveland, OH
31 May 2025

17372634R00184